AN OFFICER, NOT A GENTLEMAN

ELIZABETH JOHNS

PROLOGUE

Vitoria, Northern Spain, June 1813
The Allied Encampment

*T*he grief was so thick in their throats, none could speak. They had been together for only two years, yet the bonds of the battle were forged stronger than any created by blood. It was not something that could be explained, only experienced.

When they had set sail from England for the Peninsula, each had felt invincible, ready to conquer evil and save England. Now, it was hard to remember why they needed to be brave any more.

There was a chill in the air as they all sat huddled around the fire. James shivered. The silence the night before a battle was eerie, but afterwards, it was deafening. Watching the campfire's flames perform their blue, gold and orange dance, it did not seem real that one of them was gone. They had survived Ciudad Rodrigo, Badajoz, and Salamanca, yet Peter had fallen before their eyes today. His sabre had been raised and his eyes fierce, ready to charge when a shot had seared through him. He was on his horse one moment and gone the next. The scene replayed over and over in their minds in slow-motion. Memory was a cruel, cruel master. The same battle had left Luke wounded when a shell exploded near him. He had insisted on joining them tonight, eschewing the orders of the sawbones and hobbling out of the medical tent on the arm of his batman, Tobin.

Now, there were six of them left, if Peter's widow was included, and all wondered, *Was this to be their fate?*

Someone had to speak and break the chain of their morbid, damning thoughts.

"Peter would not want this." Four pairs of morose eyes looked up at Matthias. "We all knew this was likely when we signed up to fight Napoleon."

"How would you want us to feel if it were you?" James asked.

"I would want you to keep going and give my life meaning."

"Precisely. We mourn this night and move forward tomorrow. His death shall not be in vain," James said with quiet conviction.

"I still do not understand how we were caught unawares. Unless..." Colin was replaying the scene over in his mind.

"Someone gave our position away." Luke voiced what they all suspected.

"We were ambushed," Matthias added. In the end, England had emerged the victor, but it had been a near thing.

"What about Kitty?" Peter's wife followed the drum and felt like one of them.

"We see what she wishes to do. I expect she will wish to return home," Matthias answered. He had known her and Peter from the cradle and was the most devastated by the loss.

"The French are worn down; this cannot go on much longer," Luke said, though he would be sent home. No one else dared voice such hope.

"We are worn down," James muttered.

Philip, the quiet, thoughtful one, spoke. "If anything happens to me, will someone look to my sister? She has no one else."

"I swear it," Colin said, leading the others to do the same.

"*Pietas et honos.*"

Philip nodded, too affected to speak.

"Loyalty and honour." Another swore the oath in English.

They returned to silence, each brooding over what had happened and what was yet to come.

CHAPTER 1

Brussels, Belgium Spring 1815

Something big was brewing, Tobin could feel it in his bones. The tyrant, Napoleon, had escaped his captivity—if one could call it captivity. Some tomfool had had the daft notion of allowing Napoleon to live on an island and rule it... and people were surprised when he escaped?

"The ejeets," he muttered.

"What was that, Lieutenant?"

"Nothing, sir."

"Speaking to yourself again, O'Neill?" His commanding officer looked up from his desk with a twinkle in his eye.

"Yes, sir. It is very cathartic, sir."

"If you say so."

Tobin smiled. He still could not believe he was an officer now, and serving on Wellington's staff at that. Tobin's former master, the Duke of Waverley, had bought him a commission on a whim so he could help search for one of their lost brethren, as the group of soldiers liked to style themselves. It had turned out that the missing man was not lost after all, but on a secret mission for Wellington. Captain Elliot and he still worked secretively for the Field Marshal when necessary. It had been exciting and entertaining at times, but there had been an air of fear that had hung about them with wondering what Napoleon would do.

Wellington had been none too pleased when he discovered Tobin's part in destroying the munitions hidden in Napoleon's mistress's cave in France. He had ordered his officers to leave them alone. Had it not been for the Duke of Waverley and Lady Amelia Blake, *nee* Elliot, taking responsibility, he would be in the stocks. Instead, he was stationed in Brussels, still Lieutenant O'Neill, and serving on Wellington's staff.

Napoleon had escaped Elba, as they had foreseen some months ago, and was even now reported to be in France, amassing an army. Tobin would like to think they would be less prepared due to his efforts against La Glacier, Napoleon's ex-mistress, but time would tell.

Wellington was himself amassing his troops near Brussels, expecting the battle to occur near there. No one questioned if there would be a battle, only when and where it would happen.

It seemed London Society found it thrilling, for many of the *ton* had flocked to Brussels as soon as they had heard. Tobin would never understand them. He still did not feel comfortable—or belong—amongst them.

Waverley, still involved in the military through politics, had even come with his wife and sister, to support them however they may, and Captain Elliot was still a serving officer.

"Will you be joining us this evening, O'Neill?" Captain Murphy asked.

"The Duchess would have my head if I did not," Tobin retorted.

"But will you actually dance instead of skulking in the corner? Don't let Hooky catch you at it."

Tobin groaned. He did not understand why the nobs liked to prance about in dancing slippers. "If you wish to mince about like a molly, Murphy."

"I will wager you fifty guineas that you will be forced to dance tonight."

"Wellington requires it of all of his officers, Tobin," put in Sir Charles Stuart, having overheard the conversation whilst approaching from the next room. "Do not accept a wager you cannot win."

Captain Campbell gave a half shrug. "That's unsporting of you, sir!"

"As much as trying to gammon our green lieutenant."

Tobin grinned at Campbell. He could not complain about any of the officers he served with on Wellington's staff. They had been uncommonly accepting of him with his plebeian Irish origins. He had been a batman, for goodness' sake.

"You had better go and start polishing your boots, O'Neill."

Tobin cursed at Campbell in Gaelic even though he was fond of him. He knew the ribbing was good-natured.

"I will make certain his Grace does not have anything more urgent for me to do before I haul my own bathwater, polish my boots and brush my coat."

"My father and sister have arrived from Vienna with Wellington. I would like to introduce you to them tonight. Promise me you will ask my sister to dance if she is a wallflower."

"That was almost underhanded, Campbell. Wagering I would be forced to dance, then asking me to partner your sister. However, you should respect your sister's toes and dignity more."

His friend smiled and winked at him as Tobin put on his hat to leave Headquarters.

Wellington was nowhere to be found, so Tobin went out into the beautiful spring weather and strolled the few streets to where the Duke and Duchess of Waverley had taken a house on the Rue de Loi. Normally, Tobin would have quartered with Wellington's staff, but there were so many of Society there in Brussels that those who had family stayed with them.

As Tobin walked across Le Parc, he still could not but wonder about how swells could hold balls when war was on their doorstep.

Wellington always said it kept the men's minds diverted. "One cannot war all of the time."

Perhaps it did. Tobin would never understand. Now he was caught between the two worlds. He was no longer a servant, yet he would never be a gentleman. When he had been invited to Wellington's staff, the great man himself had reminded Tobin that he himself was Irish. When Tobin had argued he was not a gentleman, the Duke had merely said, "Because a man is born in a stable, it does not make him a horse."

And that had been that.

When Tobin arrived at the large, white stone house, the outside looked calm with bright blooms pouring from its terrace baskets in pinks and reds. Inside, it was at sixes and sevens, as one would expect on the day of a ball. No one noticed Tobin walk in. As he made his way to his rooms, he passed the ballroom, which was fragrant with the pots of fresh flowers that stood about the room in between the long windows. The candelabras were ready to be lit and raised, even though at this time of the year the hour would be late when darkness fell. A soft breeze was wafting through the open terrace doors, but it would be stuffy in there very soon, once the crush of Society present in Brussels descended. Tobin dreaded it. He hated crowds and he hated the hot dress regimentals—even though he was beyond proud to wear them.

"Tobin!" A familiar voice sounded. He turned to see The Duchess of Waverley coming towards him, still exotically beautiful with her pale blond hair and ice-blue eyes, despite having given birth only a few months ago.

He bowed. "Your Grace."

"I am so glad you are returned early! I wanted to make certain you would be here for dinner."

"I always make certain I am home for dinner," he replied cheekily, knowing that was not what she meant.

"There was a last-minute cancellation and I need you to have dinner with us. I know you hate it, but I need you. Please, Tobin."

How could he say no to her?

"Ver' well, if you insist, but do not blame me if I use the wrong fork."

She gave him a look of amused tolerance before kissing him on the cheek. "I knew you would not fail me. I must go and dress now."

Tobin cursed at himself for showing his face before the dinner had begun. He turned and made his way up the stairs to his apartment. The Duchess insisted he occupy a guest bedchamber while they were in residence.

Tobin would have preferred to have a dram of whiskey and stay in his room for the night, but instead he pulled his regimentals from the wardrobe and prepared to put them on. How many times he had done this for the Duke, he could not number, but this time was for himself. The other officers all had valets or batmen to assist them, but it did not seem right to Tobin when he could just as easily do for himself. He had been them.

Brushing the fine wool jacket, then ensuring his boots were polished better than any other officers would be, he dressed and then waited until the last possible moment to go downstairs to the drawing room. Murphy has been right about one thing: Tobin would skulk in the corner where he belonged.

When he entered the room, the Duchess gave him a knowing look and the Duke made his way over to greet him.

"Good evening, Tobin. Her Grace was about to send me to haul you down here by your ear."

"*Gommeril*," Tobin muttered.

"Are there any introductions that need to be made? You cannot go into the dining room otherwise. You might be seated by a lady with whom you could not speak," he said, ignoring Tobin's curse.

"You canna' be serious!" Tobin exclaimed, letting his Irish brogue loose. He had learned to contain it for the most part, except when he was out of sorts.

"General Dónal Murphy and his daughter have just arrived from Vienna. You are not acquainted, are you?"

"Not yet."

At that moment, Captain Murphy caught Tobin's eye and gave a wave.

Waverley led Tobin over to them. "They have taken the house next to us," Waverley informed him as they walked across the room.

"Father, I would like to introduce you to another officer on staff with me, Lieutenant O'Neill. Tobin, this is my father, General Murphy, and this is my sister, Bridget."

Tobin bowed and looked up into the face of an Irish fairy. Dark blue eyes and ebony locks surrounded a cherubic face. Tobin, for once, was bereft of words. He felt a gentle nudge in his back and bowed again.

"It is a pleasure to meet you, sir... miss," he managed to say.

He looked again towards that sweet face, so perfect, and knew it was beyond his touch, yet he could still do something for her. He could fight the war and keep the barbarians away from her.

"I do not think my sister yet has a full dance card, do you, Bridget?"

She smiled with a flash of annoyance at her brother and Tobin he knew he would spend the entire evening prancing about were she to ask it of him.

"I will do you no credit on the floor, lass, but I would not have you sit along the wall if your heart's desire is to dance."

"It is now," she whispered.

Her response surprised Tobin and their eyes met. He was a daft fool, sinking into quicksand.

BRIDGET NEVER FELT QUITE AS if she belonged at these Society parties. Her father was a gentleman and, she supposed, important in the army, but she had been brought up without a mother, following the drum, and she did not quite fit in. Most of the people who were in Brussels meant well, and had some familiar connection to the army, but they still did not understand what army life was like. Her father tried to make sure she had the latest fashions, so Bridget was wearing a beautiful ball gown in dark green and knew she looked the part. None-theless, she felt like a child's doll on display. She considered herself a nurse; even though the army had no such position, they should. During every single battle she was needed to help, and she was quite competent now, having done it for so many years.

Now, after years of watching soldiers die, she knew they faced the biggest battle yet. Never would she be able to completely numb herself to the emotion of losing people she cared about, but she was able to do what she must when she had to without simpering or swooning. Although her father was urging her to marry, for she was quite upon the shelf at five-and-twenty, Bridget knew there was little likelihood of finding someone, except perhaps a career officer who would take her as she was. Once, there had been a promising young captain, but the Battle of Badajoz had claimed him and Bridget had not wanted to risk losing her heart again. Perhaps she could find someone to make her comfortable so she would not be a burden on her father.

They had just arrived in Brussels, alongside Wellington, to prepare for the expected battle against Napoleon and the French. Instead of setting up the house, Bridget had been informed she was invited to a ball at the house next door almost as soon as her brother had greeted her on the steps.

"I am tired, Patrick. May I not be excused tonight?" she asked, offering her cheek for a kiss.

"But I have friends I wish you to meet. You will like them. They are not high in the instep at all, and it is only next door, so you may cry off early if you wish."

"Who are these paragons?" she asked, growing resigned. She knew Papa would insist that she go if Patrick told him to.

"You should remember Major Waverley. He and his wife are hosting the ball. Her sister married Captain Elliot and means to follow the drum."

Bridget smiled. She quite liked Captain Elliot. He was a horrid flirt, but she had never felt threatened by him or more than brotherly affection for him. "I hope she is worthy of him."

"It would seem so, but I know he would appreciate it if you would befriend her and show her how to go on. No doubt the Duke will wish to take the Duchess and the babe back to England soon."

"It would be my pleasure," she replied.

Now she stood in the ballroom, in a sea of red-uniformed officers, most of whom she recognized, with a few of the Rifles' green and the Cavalry's blue. Her father was speaking with his peers about the impending battle and speculating about what Boney might do. Wellington was close-lipped, as usual, and Bridget smiled and nodded when required. Rarely was her conversation necessary at these events.

Her brother had moved back to their side and she saw him hail someone across the crowded room. Soon, the Duke and a lieutenant were walking their way.

The man looked slightly familiar, but Bridget's pulse suddenly began to throb and she felt self-conscious about her appearance for the first time she could remember. That was many moons ago.

"Gracious, Bridget," she chided herself.

When his deep green eyes met hers and he was introduced as Lieutenant O'Neill, he opened his mouth and a delicious Irish brogue charmed her ears. Propriety be hanged; she was on the shelf and she meant at least to enjoy dancing with this handsome Irishman. His manner and smile proclaimed he was rake, scoundrel and rascal all in one beautiful package, and suddenly she knew she wanted to savour him, morsel by morsel.

Indeed, her brother was as good as announcing her spinsterhood and desperation to the man by soliciting dances for her.

The man then said, in the musical brogue that she could listen to all day, "I will do you no credit on the floor, lass, but I would not have you sit along the wall if your heart's desire is to dance."

Bridget thought she did not care if she danced or not, but her words betrayed her.

"It is now," she whispered.

She knew she was a fool, but anyone following the drum knew that life was short. If she had the chance for even a moment of happiness, she would seize it.

Lines began to form for the opening set, and musicians began to strum a tune. Lieutenant O'Neill looked like a fish out of water, but she took his arm, not ready to let him go. She cast a smile at her father, who was suddenly paying attention since she was dancing with a partner of her own free will. She smiled impudently at him and then followed the lieutenant towards the floor.

"I must apologize in advance, miss."

"Are you really so poor a dancer as that?" she asked.

"I used to dance with my mam and sister years ago, and the fellows have been making me twirl about to make his Grace happy, but I confess, I feel ridiculous doing it."

She laughed heartily and she had to force it back when others began looking their way.

The dance began and Lieutenant O'Neill was not so clumsy as he professed. While it was true he seemed to be concentrating overly much, he was not stepping on her toes or mincing about as a fop as he evidently feared.

"You look familiar, sir. Where might I know you from?"

"I was Waverley's batman before he purchased a commission for me." He watched her closely in his confession, and Bridget vowed not to show any sign of horror.

"You have done well for yourself. I bet your mam is proud. I honour any soldier who advances on his own merit."

"My mam would have said I am putting on airs above my station, is what. I do not belong in this world," he countered.

"I think it says much about your character that your former commander thought you could be an officer. Not only that, Wellington chose you to serve on his staff."

Clearly the lieutenant did not appreciate the praise. His face took on a heavy scowl and Bridget was afraid she had offended him deeply.

When their steps rejoined in the dance, he changed the subject. "Your name is Irish," he stated. Although there was no tone of query, she felt obliged to explain.

"My mother was Irish. My father is as well, though you might not ever know it unless he told you."

"Much like Wellington," he agreed.

"My mother died when I was four, from dysentery during one of the campaigns. I have travelled alone with Papa ever since."

"He must enjoy having you to look after him."

"He despairs of me," Bridget said with a laugh.

Lieutenant O'Neill frowned. Now what had she said?

"He desires for me to marry and live the docile life of a lady in England."

"I cannot say that I disagree with him."

"I grow bored just thinking of it," she said frankly. "I consider myself a career soldier in a dress, sir. I may not march at the drums or carry a rifle, but I do my duty just the same."

He watched her closely as they made a turn in the middle of a group. She continued quickly, "I cook, I sew, I nurse. I worry every time they leave who will come back. I can tell you, sir, I would much rather be in your boots on the front lines." She shook her head. "Forgive me, I grow passionate."

"Never apologize, ma'am. You are right, of course, though you are much prettier than any soldier I have ever met."

Bridget tried not to show her pleasure at his words and cast a mocking glare at him. The dance was drawing to a close, and she did not want her time with him to be over.

"You have not stepped on my toes once, sir."

"A happy coincidence, I assure you," he countered as she took his arm to leave the floor.

"I believe I am still in need of a partner for the waltz," she said brazenly.

"I would not press my luck twice in one night," he said, eyes wide.

"You would make me dance with my father or brother then." She almost cringed at her desperation.

"How could I cause a lady such distress? Very well, but I give you and your toes fair warning, *mo álainn*."

CHAPTER 2

*G*o home now, Lieutenant," Wellington ordered.

Tobin glanced up to see the Duke standing before him, looking displeased. He immediately rose to his feet. "Sir, I have a few more reports to prepare."

"Nothing that cannot wait until tomorrow, I'll warrant. There will be enough wearing yourself thin once the battle begins. I appreciate your efforts, but go home. The rest of the lads left hours ago. You should be out charming the ladies. That is what I intend to do, Lieutenant."

"Yes, sir." Tobin gathered his papers into a neat pile and picked his bicorne hat up from a hook on the wall. The fact was, he did not want to go home; the chances of seeing Bridget Murphy were too high. He would either be coaxed into some social activity or come across her in the park. There was no sense in torturing himself by seeing her again. It had been a mistake to dance with her and waltz with her. It was like dangling a large piece of fish in front of a starving cat and expecting it to not take a bite.

He began the tramp back to the house, walking through the park. He enjoyed seeing the children play with their mothers and nurses; the lush green grass, trees and flowers. He could almost convince himself he was a lad back in Ireland, which always made his throat thicken with emotion. This was why he fought: to protect these innocents from evil. Did they know war was almost upon them?

"Of course not," he muttered and shook his head, dipping his fingers into the cold water of a fountain as he passed.

"Do you often talk to yourself?"

He heard her angelic voice with the slight Irish lilt to it, yet had not noticed her approach. *Shocking admission for a soldier*, he thought.

He did not look up. "Often," he said, smiling to himself.

"I like to come here to think," she said, without really greeting him. He liked that she was not so formal. Though he knew he should greet her properly, he did not wish to spoil the moment.

"Why are you not at a fancy party or dinner?" he asked softly over the melody of the fountain's soothing trickle.

"They are not really to my taste," she said with a slight laugh and he had to look up at her.

Beggorah, she was beautiful. "I canna' fash why not," he said, not bothering to hide his brogue around her. It was a relief to be himself.

"I could ask you the same question. Why are you not out charming the ladies who came here just for a dance with a handsome man in a dashing uniform?"

Tobin laughed. "Ask your brother. I prefer to hold up the walls in the corner."

"Then I should feel doubly honoured that you danced twice with me."

"The honour was all mine," he said, looking to her eyes and feeling lost.

"You are different," she pronounced. "Not just because you are Irish and not just because you were a batman."

"I am happy to be different, if that is what ye like." He smiled.

She smiled back. "I am different, too."

"Ye are perfect, *mo álainn*."

She sat down on the edge of the fountain and held her hand out for him to join her.

Cautiously he sat next to her. "Why are you out here all alone? Should you not have a maid or someone to protect you?"

She laughed derisively. "What could a maid do? I am an ape leader and I follow the drum. I do not have a chaperone when we are in camp. Must everything be different because some members of London Society came to watch the battle, as if it were a performing circus?"

"I have always thought many of the rules were ridiculous, myself, but I do know what people are capable of and I would like to think that you were safe."

"From men like you?" she whispered, looking up into his eyes.

"Most definitely from men like me." He was quickly losing control of this conversation. There was a reason he had been working long hours to avoid her.

"I am not afraid of you, Lieutenant." She ran her fingers through the water as he had done a few minutes ago. There was something so beautiful about an ungloved hand and it was mesmerizing to watch the water trickle through each finger.

She should be afraid. In her company, Tobin was afraid of himself.

"Will you walk with me?" she asked.

"Where are your father and brother?" He stood when she did and she placed her hand on his arm.

"At a dinner or party. I told you, I do not enjoy such things. I often stay behind."

"Then why were you at the ball three nights ago?" He looked down at her.

"You should not scowl like that, Lieutenant."

He tried to soften his features. "Better, *mo álainn*?"

She tilted one side of her mouth up in a smile. "Yes."

He might as well plunge his head in the fountain now, because he was drowning.

"To answer your question, Patrick insisted I attend. He said he had someone he wanted me to meet." She looked at him pointedly.

"Me?"

"You and Mrs. Elliot. He asked me to befriend her and show her how to be an army wife."

"Ah, the Lady Amelia."

"Do you know her well?"

"Very well. We worked together, in a fashion. You will like her, though she is no conforming miss. Captain Elliot has his hands full. I never saw a lady up to such mischief."

"They should suit well, then," she agreed with a laugh.

They walked in comfortable silence along several tree-lined paths. The sun was beginning to lower in the sky, casting a violet-pink hue over the horizon.

"This is my favourite time of day. I love sunrise as well, but everything seems more intense at sunset: the warmth, the smells, the colours and the sounds."

Tobin would never see sunsets the same way again.

"Are you always so quiet, Lieutenant? Not that I mind. I feel a kinship with you. May I call you friend?"

"Ye may call me whatever ye wish, *mo álainn*."

She stopped and turned to him, laughing. "Thank you. I have not enjoyed an evening so much in a long while."

"I canna' say I have ever."

"Will you join us tomorrow on a picnic? Please say you will not leave me to face all of them alone."

"Ye are one of them, *mo álainn*. I am the one who should not have to face them. Besides, we are still working. I canna' run away at my leisure."

"Patrick and Captain Elliot plan to attend, so I think you are making excuses, sir."

"I will ask permission, but I make no promises as the lowly lieutenant. There is still much to be done."

She was silent for a few minutes as they walked along, the crunch of gravel sounding beneath their boots. "How soon?" she asked.

He did not pretend to mistake her meaning. "We do not know for sure. Within a week would be my best guess."

She nodded her head, biting her lower lip. "I had heard people were beginning to flee the city."

"And you? Where will you go?"

"Where I always go—to help. I either set up our house as a hospital or, if needed, I go to one of the infirmary tents. I have been doing so since I was fourteen."

He looked at her with new respect. "You meant it when you said you were a nurse."

She nodded. "I had better prepare in earnest. Patrick and Father fear this will be one of the biggest battles to date."

"I am afraid I agree. But Napoleon must be stopped."

"Yes," she whispered.

Tobin turned them back towards the Rue de Loi since the sun had almost set. To Tobin, it had been the most perfect evening he had ever known. Repeating it must be avoided at all costs, he told himself, although he knew he could never refuse her anything. In his eyes, she was the perfect combination of beauty and womanhood. She was peaceful. He had never thought a person could be peaceful—it was a strange sensation.

When they reached the street again, Tobin found it hard to let her go.

"I will see you tomorrow, Lieutenant."

"That was not a question, lass. You know I must ask my superior."

She gave him a look to melt his hardened insides, then turned and walked up the steps to her house. He watched her go and stood there long after the door had closed behind her. It was an evening he would treasure always, and he knew Bridget Murphy would fill his dreams for years to come, but she was a lady. He was not fit to kiss her hem.

BRIDGET WAS SURPRISED to find her father at home when she came through the front door.

"Papa! I thought you had gone to the card party with Patrick."

"I did. I came home early. Have you been out alone at this late hour?"

"I was, but I met Lieutenant O'Neil on his way home and we

walked together for a while."

He frowned at her. "Was that wise? What do you know of him? I know he is on Wellington's staff, which says much, but I have never heard of his family."

"I do not think he comes from any noble family, if that is what you are asking."

"Promise me you will be careful, Bridget," he said in warning tones.

"I will, Father."

"You know I only wish for your happiness. I do not know how you will find it while following the drum. There is not much happiness to be found in the business of war."

"I am aware of the life, Papa. You are morose because there is a battle coming. You are always affected so." She looked at him affectionately.

"You know me well, daughter. I want you also to know that if something were to happen to Patrick and me, you will be provided for." His tone was melancholy.

"I know, Papa. I do not wish to speak of it. Nor do I wish you to beg me to remove myself to my aunt's house."

He chuckled and shook his head. "You are the one who should have been a general."

"I cannot argue with that." She grinned back.

"I do like that this Lieutenant O'Neil brings a smile to your face, but I would wish for you to marry someone of your station. You must think of your future and your children, Bridget. It is easy to mistake your feelings with the threat of battle imminent. Please do not do anything you will regret."

"I won't. Good night, Papa," she said, kissing him on the forehead. There was no point in arguing with him lest he forbid her to see the lieutenant all together. Perhaps it was a guilty pleasure, but it was one she would not want to deny herself.

The next morning, the anticipation Bridget felt was more than was warranted by a simple picnic with friends. She dressed with more careful attention than usual, and she made certain the preparations were perfect. Lady Amelia Elliot had suggested the picnic, and Bridget had agreed to help with the arrangements. The carriages were drawn up at the front of the house, the ladies were ready and the baskets loaded, but the three officers kept them waiting.

"Do you think they will not come?" Amelia asked, growing obviously impatient.

"I think they are here on military duty, and we must await their pleasure, if they are to have any," the Duke replied with a twinge of reprimand.

"It is the way of things, unfortunately," Bridget agreed. "It would not be the first time my plans were thwarted."

"I suspect they will be here soon or they would have sent a note," the Duchess added, so they waited.

It was a warm but cloudy day, the threat of rain often present here in the spring as it was in England. They waited near the open carriages and Bridget felt herself grow more impatient than she should have. They were joined by Lady Georgiana Lennox, who was riding along with them. Bridget presumed her ladyship had accompanied them in order to meet her brother and another party, who was to join them there, but they were not close acquaintances.

It was another half an hour before the three officers arrived. Captain Elliot, along with her brother and Lieutenant O'Neill, walked toward them from the park, a fine display of British manhood.

"Forgive our tardiness," Captain Elliot said with a bow to the ladies. "It was a near thing for Wellington to allow O'Neill to escape, and then only after an important dispatch was delivered."

"We are grateful to have you, Tobin," the Duchess said fondly.

It was curious, Bridget thought, as she watched Lieutenant O'Neill with the Duke and Duchess, that they certainly treated him more like family than an old servant.

"We should be on our way before the rain decides to join our party," Lady Amelia suggested.

Bridget climbed into the open carriage and was joined by Lieutenant O'Neill, Captain Elliot and his wife. Bridget would not complain; it was just as she had hoped.

"You will be interested to know that our brethren have all arrived, even Thackeray," Elliot said to Lieutenant O'Neill.

"I have not seen them since your wedding. Thackeray decided to join in the fight again, eh?"

"Strictly on a volunteer basis," Elliot answered, "much to the chagrin of those who sit in their neat, comfortable clubs back in London."

Lieutenant O'Neill muttered something under his breath. It was the dearest little habit of his, Bridget thought.

"I remember the brethren," she remarked. "You were as thick as thieves, if I remember correctly."

"We lost Peter at Vitoria, then Waverley was injured and sold out," Elliot explained.

"Then he had the daft idea to purchase me a commission," O'Neill teased.

"You came to my rescue twice, Tobin," Amelia retorted, "and he did it so you could look for Philip. I think you will do."

"What is your opinion of following the drum, so far?" Bridget asked Lady Amelia.

"I do not think being quartered in Brussels is a fair taste," she answered.

"Not yet, no. I am going into town tomorrow, to begin gathering supplies, if you would like to help me. You may not wish to assist with nursing, but there are many things you may do to help without dirtying your hands."

"If you did not wish for her help, you said the wrong thing," Captain Elliot interjected into their conversation, a twinkle in his eye.

"Yes, indeed," Lady Amelia agreed with a reciprocal twinkle. She leaned forward as though imparting a secret. "I am not very adept at behaving like a proper lady."

Lieutenant O'Neill let out a guffaw. "Saints above, that is an understatement."

Lady Amelia simply returned with a cheeky look bearing pride and affection.

"Miss Murphy is a very competent nurse. I wish we had a force of them all trained as well as she is. I am certain she could teach most of the raw sawbones a thing or two," Captain Elliot told his wife and Lieutenant O'Neill.

"Of course," Bridget said with a smile. "Nurses and doctors need to be trained just as soldiers do. Practising medicine after a battle has far different needs from those of a hypochondriac in her boudoir."

"I could prescribe smelling salts," Amelia quipped. "I confess I am fascinated. I have been wondering how I will spend my time once the men are called away."

"If you have a strong constitution, there will be more required than you or I can do, but we will do what we may, which is better than nothing."

"I would much rather look at your face than any sawbones," Tobin added.

Bridget laughed as the carriage took a track into the Soignes Forest and followed it for several hundred yards. The coachman drew the horses to a halt in a pretty spot beside a sparkling lake which the Duchess had chosen for the picnic.

Since it had been decided to do without servants, the gentlemen dutifully helped the ladies carry the hampers and spread blankets on the ground beneath a canopy of beech trees along the water. The ladies then passed out plates of food.

A delectable array of dishes was set out before them, including Château d'Arville, Fromage de Bruxelles, and Passchendaele cheeses served with crackers; waffles with cubes of sugar baked inside and served with fresh berries and cream; sandwiches of ham and egg all complimented with light wines and ale.

"It is much more comfortable to have the ladies with us," Captain Elliot mused.

"I suppose so. We never had any fancy picnics before," Lieutenant O'Neill replied before biting into a chicken leg.

"If only this were all it was," Bridget said softly. "Forgive me, I do not mean to put a damper on the lovely afternoon. I have never been good at turning the soldier on and off."

"Wellington is the master, is he not?" the Duke put in. "I used to grow very frustrated with his notion that we fight by day and dance by night."

"I confess, it is why I do not wish to enter Society in England, having been brought up following the army from battle to battle. I admire people who can reintegrate so easily, but I am not one," Bridget said softly.

Lady Amelia smiled at her. "I do not know if I will be able to adapt, myself. I have never been good at conforming to the rules. I was bred to pretend nothing affected me and smile..."

Her husband nearly choked on his drink but she ignored him.

"I will depend upon you to show me how to go on, Miss Murphy."

"I would be delighted. We always need extra hands, Lady Amelia."

The others began their own conversations, and some of the gentlemen rowed ladies out in boats and others chose to fish. Bridget could feel the lieutenant's eyes on her. She turned to look at him, questioning.

"Tell me about it," he said. "Do you go into the field?"

"Sometimes, but never during the fighting. I help gather supplies, because there are never enough, and afterwards I help tend to the invalids."

"I was fortunate in my time with the army before. I only gained a few scratches."

"I pray it will remain the same, Lieutenant." She looked him in the eye and knew he understood.

"It is near," he said softly.

Bridget nodded, knowing it was true. "Then may we enjoy the time we can. Will you walk with me?" She could feel his reluctance, and she knew why. It had been her own reasoning for keeping gentlemen at a distance before.

They walked along beside the water, the tall grasses and bulrush providing shelter for a skein of ducklings while some swans glided gracefully nearby. Saying very little, they enjoyed tranquil silence much as they had in the Park as nature happened around them. It was something Bridget would treasure always.

CHAPTER 3

*I*t was strange, waging war the gentlemanly way. Before, when he had been a batman, Tobin had always been with the enlisted folk or other servants. Not that the Duke had ever treated him inferiorly—quite the contrary, in fact. However, now he was treated like a gentleman and expected to behave as one. He had chambers on the same floor as the family and sat at the table with them. Every morning since their arrival in Brussels, he had walked to Headquarters with Captain Elliot and Captain Murphy. Today was to be a military review, where all of the troops would be on display for their commander's perusal. It was to be a grand show, indeed. Tobin had never had the luxury of being on display at any of these parades before, always taking up the rear.

Now, he had a beautiful black stallion, Trojan, who had been handed on to him by the Duke of Waverley. He was well trained for battle and the Duke had said he was wasted in his stables in England.

As Tobin joined Elliot and Murphy, who were mounting their horses to ride to the review, he wondered if they thought him as big a fraud as he felt.

"I am jealous Luke allowed you to have Trojan," Captain Elliot said as he watched Tobin mount.

"He knew I could handle him," Tobin replied with his usual cheek.

Captain Murphy chuckled. "Now I know why my sister likes you."

She likes me? Tobin wondered. That remark indicated they had discussed him.

"Bridget despises pretension. I am grateful you were able to draw her out at the ball."

"I would think you would rather pluck my eyes out," Tobin said candidly.

"Bridget's life has not been hers to live. She will protest that she would have it no other way, but it is hard on her. Any amusement or happiness she can find for herself, I welcome."

Tobin was stunned.

"I am glad she will be here to help Amelia. I know we are serving on staff this battle, but there are never any guarantees," Captain Elliot added.

"I would not say this in front of Bridget, and I know Lady Amelia has family to care for her should something happen, but I would like to know someone would look after my sister should something happen to me and my father. Our only other family is an elderly aunt and she is not someone you would choose to know."

"Of course, you have my word," Captain Elliot said quickly.

Murphy looked at Tobin. "Of course. I will do everything in my power to help," he responded.

"Thank you." Murphy nodded. They said little else as they negotiated their horses through the traffic and out to the picturesque riverbank of the Dender near Grammont.

Soon, they met up with Matthias, Lord Thackeray, James, Captain Frome, and Colin, Major White.

"It will not be the same without all of us together," Philip said.

"Yes, enjoy your luxurious positions on staff, while the real officers hold the line," James teased.

"We will still be protecting your sorry arse," Tobin muttered.

"I will take that in the way it was intended," Colin said. "I still remember how you saved Waverley that time at Ciudad Rodrigo.

Someone had taken Peter out, and if you had not shot the cuirassier off his horse, he would have shot the Duke."

Tobin did not want to receive praise for what was his duty. Instead he looked over to Thackeray.

"They let you out of your castle, eh?"

"I have two younger brothers. You could not keep me away. We should have put Boney away properly the first time."

All of them murmured their agreement.

"You look good wearing the pips," Thackeray said, acknowledging Tobin's rank.

An open carriage pulled up beside them, holding the Duke and Duchess, Lady Amelia and Miss Murphy. Tobin would be lying if he said he was not affected by her presence. She looked like a bright summer day in a simple jonquil muslin, her hair tucked beneath a straw-chip bonnet with a couple of daisies intertwined with a ribbon. He wanted to pluck her from the carriage and take her to the meadow.

"Speak of the devil," Colin said.

"I am quite jealous of you, Tobin," the Duke said, looking fondly over his brethren and horse.

"I will take good care of Trojan, Major." As he spoke, the horse sidled over to greet his former master.

"You were a good soldier, Trojan," the Duke said, patting his charger's nose. "But now you must do the same for Tobin."

Tobin's eyes met Miss Murphy's and he doffed his hat to her. "Greetings, ladies."

"We had better be on our way. Wellington would not take kindly to his staff arriving late," Captain Elliot reminded them.

As a group, the brethren rode on in front of the carriage, Tobin consciously aware of Miss Murphy behind him. So what if he sat a little straighter and prouder in his saddle—who would know beyond himself? They joined the thousands of soldiers and cavalrymen, James, Colin and Thackeray departing to parade with their battalion.

Wellington joined them some minutes later, along with Blucher, and the assembled followed through the pomp and circumstance of the review. The cavalry went first, including the Guards, then the infantry. Tobin knew how important the display was for the morale of the troops. Seeing that the army was large and grand would give them confidence ahead of the big day like nothing else would. It certainly made it feel real to Tobin. It would not hurt, he thought, for word to reach Napoleon's ears, a likely possibility since all of Brussels appeared to have come to watch.

After Wellington was satisfied, the soldiers were released to their commanders for drill. Tobin, Murphy and Elliot returned to say farewell to those in the carriage before returning to Headquarters. It was quite the social event, Tobin mused. He had not particularly noticed how fine the ladies were dressed before, but now, seeing all the carriages full of ladies, with their fancy bonnets and parasols, and gentlemen in their smartest, Tobin really had to shake his head at the ways of the *beau monde*.

"It seems ridiculous, does it not?"

Tobin turned at the sound of Miss Murphy's voice.

"Are my thoughts so obvious?" he asked, surprised at his response to her.

"I confess I preferred the Peninsular campaign. That did not resemble a small Season in London. Nevertheless, I am glad if people's families can be here to provide comfort."

"Or distraction," he retorted, drawing a smile from her.

"I will not tell anyone our true feelings," she said, her eyes still twinkling.

"I suspect most of these people will leave soon. Reports are starting to come in that the French are advancing."

Miss Murphy nodded. "It will be just as well if they leave. I must begin my preparations when we return to town. These ladies have agreed to help me."

"Waverley is staying?"

"For now, apparently."

"I suppose he has his own carriage and horses and can leave when he wishes," he reflected.

"Will you be attending The Duchess of Richmond's ball?" she asked.

"Not if I can help it," he teased.

"If only I can be so fortunate." She pretended to pout.

"You are not a typical lady, *mo álainn*."

"Much to my father's chagrin," she agreed with a laugh.

"We had better be going," the Duke called to Tobin. "I have kept my Duchess out in the heat long enough."

"I wish you would stop fussing over me, Luke. I am perfectly well," the Duchess scolded.

"We must be returning to our duties anyway," Tobin said, winking at the Duchess.

"HE IS A ROGUE, but I adore him for it," the Duchess remarked as the carriage pulled away to cross the bridge over the river.

"It is a good thing I know the two of you are happily married," the Duke said wryly.

"Yet Miss Murphy is not," Lady Amelia added with a scheming look.

"I cannot argue with any of your statements." Bridget smiled.

Everyone laughed.

"I do hope Tobin can settle down and find happiness after this is over with," the Duchess added. "He deserves it."

"You will get no argument from me," the Duke said. "It was one of the hardest things I have ever done, to send him away."

"Do you think he is happy as an officer?" Lady Amelia asked. "Philip seems to think he is uncomfortable in the role, even though none of them view him as a former enlisted man."

"I imagine Tobin does it to himself. He would never tell you, but he is the natural son of an earl. Tobin chooses not to accept any charity, as he calls it, from him. His father tried to purchase him a commission before."

"I am glad he accepted it from you, then," the Duchess said.

"Only under duress." The Duke chuckled.

Bridget sat and listened to these highest of aristocrats speak of Lieutenant O'Neill as though he were a member of their family. She was not herself of the aristocracy, although, as a general's daughter, she had mingled with them from time to time, and her uncle had been a baron. She was quite certain Lieutenant O'Neill would be mortified to know they were speaking of him thus. She wanted to know more about him. He seemed an enigma to her. He had only ever mentioned his mam and sister, but apparently he had a rich and powerful father he shunned. He had done well for himself on his own merit.

Bridget realized Lady Amelia had asked her a question. "I beg your pardon, I was wool-gathering," she replied politely.

"I had only asked how we may be of help to you. I heard you mention to Tobin that you must begin your preparations. What exactly do you do to help during a battle?" Lady Amelia asked.

"Sometimes, very little, but frequently I help nurse the wounded. Many of the camp followers do."

"Even ladies?" the Duchess asked.

"Not all, but many do. I confess I have never been able to remain idle whilst the men are fighting. Not that it hurt that, to a fourteen-year-old girl, Dr. Craig was as handsome as a Greek god," she said, to appreciative laughter. "He gave me some of his instruments when he left the army to return to Scotland."

"And you continued helping the wounded anyway," the Duke said in a jocular tone.

"It seems the right thing to do since I have the ability. I intend to empty every apothecary's shop I may during the next few days."

"After seeing the ranks of men today and hearing that Bonaparte has over 500,000, I fear there will not be enough supplies in Europe for the carnage."

"How may we help?" Lady Amelia asked again.

"I carry trunks of blankets around with me. Warmth helps the most with shock. Boiling water ahead of time and preparing willow bark tea helps with some of the pain. Laudanum is necessary for the more severe injuries," Bridget explained, "so any of these things I can acquire or prepare beforehand is of considerable help."

"You do so much," Lady Amelia exclaimed.

"And, of course, we will require bandages. I will spend the next few days tearing flint into strips."

"Then we will tear them with you. I do not know how long we will remain in Brussels. If the fighting gets too close, we will leave, but we are at your disposal until then," the Duchess assured her.

"I intend to stay. Where do they put the wounded?" Lady Amelia asked. "Are there tents set up for them?"

"It depends on the battle. Usually there are tents on the edges of the battlefields for the most dire cases, but I suspect many of the wounded will need to be cared for here, in Brussels. I intend to make our house available."

"I will keep ours if you think it would help," the Duke said. "In fact, I know it will help. I have been one of the wounded at the mercy of the sawbones."

As they drove back into town, at every apothecary or shop they passed which the Duke thought might have the supplies they sought, he stopped and bought all he could.

By the time they returned to the house, each lady's arms were overflowing with blankets, bandages or medicines. Bridget laughed at the enormity of the Duke's purchases and accepted their invitation to take tea and begin working on the preparations. A nurse soon brought down their young infant, Lady Frances, and the Duke held her while they organized supplies.

"I hope you do not mind, Miss Murphy," the Duke said sheepishly. "When you reminded me of my own injury and the person who saved my leg, I suddenly felt the need to do what I could."

"How could I complain? You have saved me a great deal of shopping!"

"That is not a complaint I ever thought to hear from a lady," he quipped, "although these two sisters frequently test the bounds of what ladies should do. Do you remember the time, my love, when I came home to find you picking brambles out of Tobin's... ahem... backside?"

"Of course, I remember!" she said, trying not to laugh. "I do not think Tobin would appreciate the recollection in front of his new friend, however."

"His new friend is delighted to hear it. I might need the information one day," Bridget added, relishing the mischief of the conversation.

"I have known him for ages and I might need the information," Lady Amelia chimed in, starting to giggle. Soon, both sisters were laughing, with tears streaming down their faces. "I would have given anything to witness such a scene and Luke's reaction," Lady Amelia sighed when she had recovered.

"In Tobin's defence, he was trying to rescue you, Amelia."

"But you asked him to climb the trellis in the first place, sister," Amelia retorted.

"I should not have brought it up," the Duke said, shaking his head at the feminine merriment.

It was on that note that Lieutenant O'Neill entered the house, causing all of them to burst into laughter again.

"Tobin!" the Duchess declared through her tears.

"Dare I ask?" he said, looking at Bridget for help.

"They have been telling funny stories while helping me tear and roll bandages. I had not realized the hour had grown so late. I must return home for dinner, if you have already been released for the day."

"As long as you are not leaving on my account," he replied with a devilish grin.

"If we keep telling stories about you, she will do so for certain," Amelia chimed in.

"Bad cess to ye. I wasn't actin' the maggot alone," Tobin grumbled, which sent everyone in the room into peals of laughter again.

Bridget rose to leave. "I do not know how to thank you for your help today. You barely know me, yet you have eased my burden considerably."

"We are more than happy to be useful. Besides, this should not be your burden to bear alone. We can start where we left off in the morning," the Duchess reassured her as she took her sleeping daughter from her husband's arms. "We can leave everything in here as it is for tonight."

CHAPTER 4

*T*he next two days saw Tobin and the rest of Wellington's staff bunkered down, poring over maps, writing reports and sending dispatches.

Some of the men spoke of the Duchess of Richmond's ball, which was taking place that evening, but Tobin had no intention of going to such a lavish affair. His mind was centred on the battle ahead, and from the intelligence he had gathered from his superiors, it would take a miracle for them to win this conflict. Some of the best regiments were still not returned from fighting in America, and no one was certain when the Prussians would arrive. However, Wellington, being who he was, would not allow the fact they anticipated the news to arrive at any moment to put a damper on the Duchess' festivities that night. Many of the staff had left to dress, but the only thing Tobin would be doing was having a nice meal and packing his kit.

He had always had a sixth sense, and he knew they would march out that night. He had not spoken with the Duke since the picnic, but neither was Tobin surprised to find the household packed up to leave, and the servants loading a carriage.

"Tobin," his Grace greeted him when he entered the entrance hall to see the Duke surrounded by trunks.

"I was afraid we would miss you. We are leaving to return to England, if we can manage it. I am taking only the carriage horses and will leave the others for you and Philip, should you need them."

Tobin was never one for goodbyes or displays of emotion, but the Duke meant as much to him as any brother would. He gave a swift nod, afraid to try to speak.

"Amelia will stay here with some servants and Miss Murphy will be next door. Both of them felt the houses would be very useful as makeshift hospitals."

"I will look after them," Tobin said, though there was never any question.

"You will send word?"

"Of course."

The Duke nodded and pulled Tobin into a manly hug. "I wish I could go with you."

"You have served your time, Major. From what I hear, we need you at the War Office as soon as possible."

"I will do my best. There are money and supplies in the safe should you need them. Philip also knows."

"Now, will ye be getting your Duchess and daughter on the way? I intend to bounce your babe on my knee when this is over."

"I consider that a promise, Tobin," the Duchess put in as she came down the stairs holding the little cherub.

The entrance hall was now empty of baggage, removed unobtrusively by his Grace's servants. There was nothing left to do but see them on their way.

"You intend to travel all night?" he asked the Duchess.

"I would like to be on board the ship by tomorrow morning."

"At least you have a few days' start," Tobin agreed, kissing her on the cheek.

He waved farewell as the carriage pulled forward and away down the cobbled street. He stood there until the rhythm of the horses' hooves faded and only then turned back to the house. At least Captain Elliott and Lady Amelia were still in residence or he might find himself weeping.

Tobin found Philip and Amelia finishing their dinner and about to depart for the highly anticipated ball.

"Are you not joining us?" Lady Amelia asked with a frown.

"Not tonight." His eyes met Philip's knowing ones, but neither husband nor wife said a word.

"I know you are leaving soon," Amelia declared, almost defiantly, after a moment. "I will enjoy the ball with my husband, however."

"You should," Tobin agreed. "I prefer to have a nice meal and quiet evening alone. Who knows how long it will be until the next one?"

Tobin could see tears in Amelia's eyes, but she smiled and nodded. He saw them on their way before heading to the kitchen to see what was left for a meal. Most of the servants had been hired with the house, but some had left with the Duke and Duchess.

There was plenty of roast meat, potatoes and carrots, and pudding for him to eat his fill. Afterwards, he climbed up the stairs slowly, taking in everything around him. Perhaps it was silly, but for him, everything leading up to battle seemed to be happening in slow motion, as though he were in a tunnel.

He ordered a bath, and then he very methodically folded and packed his belongings, ensuring he took what he must have if he were on his own to survive. He did not think that was very likely with this battle, but it was best to be prepared. It was very likely he would be running dispatches from place to place, and anything could happen.

Once he was ready, he lay down on the bed and rested until he heard the call, knowing that this was the eerie quiet before the storm; that it would be replaced with chaos and bloodlust once the first shot was fired.

At last, he heard horns blow, followed by the loud, repetitive thumping noise of the drums. The call to arms.

Tipping his satchel over his shoulder, he walked towards the stables. He suspected Patrick and Philip would be there shortly to retrieve their own horses, so he saddled them in anticipation, preferring to do for himself.

It would be easy to feel sorry for himself, for he had no sweetheart to wish him farewell. Previously, he had been part of a battalion that camped together and fought together.

"Are you leaving so soon?" a sweet voice asked, as though he had conjured her out of his thoughts.

He finished tightening the girth on his horse and set his head down on the saddle. "It is time," he said, wishing he could taste her sweet lips just once. He had become a romantic, he thought sardonically.

"I brought you something," she said and finally, he looked up to meet her gaze.

"You might think it is silly, but I promise they will be welcome and will hopefully make you think of me," she said with a sad smile, holding out a cloth bag to him.

"What is it?" He took the bag from her hand.

"Look and see. It is not a lock of hair, I promise."

He laughed and opened the bag. "Candies?" He looked up, surprised. "Thank you."

"You may not believe me now, but you will be thankful during the battle. Going hours without food and drink will make you happy to have one of these."

"I believe you. I don't think anyone has ever given me something quite as thoughtful."

"Father and Patrick swear by them."

"I will use them and think of the pretty face of the lady who gave them to me."

"Thank me afterwards, if you please." She stepped forward on tiptoe and placed a kiss on his cheek, almost how a sister would. If only he could think of her as a sister.

She paused, her face right next to his and he knew what she wanted, for he wanted it to. "This is not a good idea, *mo álainn*," he whispered.

"Was I mistaken? I want it very much," she said boldly, causing his resolve to turn and run straight out of the stables. He wrapped his arms around her as hers twined around his neck and their lips met. At first it was tender, but then he kissed her with the fear, desperation and abandon that a soldier tended to feel before putting on his armour and charging the enemy. She seemed to understand. She would more than any other lady would, he thought, as he tried to memorize the feel of her: how she fitted in his arms and pressed against him as though she were made for him. He drew his lips from hers, but took her face in his hands and placed kisses over her ears, her eyes, her cheeks, her neck… He could die tomorrow having at least known this.

He could die tomorrow. That crashing reality caused him to pull away.

"Do not apologize," she said. Wordlessly they stood, forehead to forehead, trying to catch their breaths.

Then, as she stepped back, Tobin gave a swift nod and brushed his hand down her cheek.

"Godspeed, Lieutenant."

CATCHING the sobs in her throat, Bridget watched Lieutenant O'Neill leave. This was not characteristic of her, but he was not like other men and she felt drawn to him. War did that to you.

She bit down on her fist to control her emotion. Memories of saying goodbye to her captain before Badajoz assailed her. This leave-taking felt remarkably similar, and she knew a deep foreboding which would not go away.

Goodbyes were the worst part, she reflected. *Well, waiting is horrible as well. Indeed, there really is no good side to war.* Sometimes, when they were encamped, she could hover on the periphery and help, but that was not possible here. There would be plenty to do, nonetheless.

She knew she would not sleep that night, after she bid her father and brother farewell, so she walked, almost absent-mindedly, to the park to watch the soldiers leave their dwellings and walk towards the south gate of the city. They were to camp that night near the small village of Waterloo. It had begun to rain and Bridget pitied the soldiers, most of whom would have no cover.

As dawn began to break, she finally returned to seek a few hours of sleep. Once the fighting began in earnest, the wounded would not stop coming because of her hunger, thirst or exhaustion.

She heard the first sounds just before noon the next morning. Cannon fire sounded like thunder and she felt a chill creep up her spine. She stopped to say prayers for each of her loved ones out there and for those she did not know—especially the scared young boys who had no choice.

Having risen and dressed, she was splashing cold water in her face when she heard a knock at the door downstairs. There were two servants left in the house with her; her father's and brother's men had gone to the field with them.

Once she had pulled a comb through her hair and bound the tresses into a tight knot, she descended the stairs to see who was calling. Lady Amelia had been admitted into the small saloon at the front of the house.

"It has begun, has it not?" Amelia asked, looking sickly pale.

"Yes. We must keep busy or we will go mad with the waiting. In a couple of hours, we can go to the Namur Gate to help. The walking wounded will begin arriving then, I expect, and that is where they plan to put makeshift tents for those able to reach this far. Some will merely need bandages and water, while some will need more serious care and may be brought back to one of our houses."

Lady Amelia swallowed hard but nodded her head.

"You will do very well. Once you get over the initial shock, you will be too busy to notice your sensibilities. Have you broken your fast? I recommend a good breakfast, for I cannot guarantee another meal today."

They removed to the breakfast parlour, where both forced themselves to eat. Bridget was more worried than usual, but she knew she must be strong for this young wife who was so new to the rigours of army life.

"What is a battle like?" Lady Amelia asked. "I assume you have seen some, even though I expect your father tries to keep you as far from harm's way as possible."

Bridget nodded. "I used to imagine there was an invisible line drawn across a field and a marshal would wave a flag, then each side would charge."

"How does it begin, then?" Lady Amelia frowned.

"Someone shoots first. Sometimes you can see the enemy, but sometimes you cannot. There is an initial charge by each side, but then the best way I can describe it is chaos. Imagine if a child threw their toy soldiers down and they scattered, and then filled the air with smoke."

"I had not considered the smoke. Can they not see until the enemy is upon them?"

"Often not, Father has told me. They try to form into squares to make them more defensible, but frequently they find themselves in hand to hand combat."

Lady Amelia looked green.

"Forgive me. I should not have been so candid."

"I did ask… and it does me no good not to know. It just makes the waiting more unbearable."

"It is why I try to stay occupied. Soon there will be dozens of wounded arriving and you will be too busy to fret."

Once they had finished some toast, eggs and tea, Bridget fetched a bag of bandages and supplies for each of them from the linen cupboard, as well as a bucket and cup they would fill at a pump near the gate. As they left the house and began their walk, it felt eerily quiet.

"Has everyone abandoned the city?"

"Many have. Many take refuge inside their houses."

"Do you think the fighting will reach here?"

"Only if we fail."

A sobering thought, which, on reflection, would have been better left unsaid, Bridget chastised herself as Lady Amelia blanched.

Bridget had calculated correctly. By the time they reached the Namur Gate, there were soldiers on foot beginning to arrive. Not serious enough to warrant the sawbones' continued attentions on the battlefield, or one of the few beds, yet they were too badly injured to continue fighting. The first young man they saw had been shot in the arm, had had the bullet dug out and been bandaged. His hand would no longer hold his rifle so, pale and sweating, he had wandered the ten miles back to town, walking as though dead on his feet. He nearly collapsed at the gate. Bridget quickly hurried to him and helped him find a place to sit in the shade. Amelia brought him a drink of water, which was what he needed most.

The soldier was no more than a boy, Bridget realized. He would be lucky if he survived the infection that was inevitable from the bullet wound.

The trickle of wounded rapidly became a deluge. Soon, there were more wounded than they could attend to quickly. Fortunately, other ladies were there to help as well. Wagon-loads of incapacitated soldiers began coming into the city. One driver stopped and called to her.

"Are you Miss Murphy?"

"I am."

"The sawbones said to bring these men to you. Do you have somewhere for them to go?"

She nodded.

"I'll take you up next to me," he said.

Bridget looked with concern at Lady Amelia, who shooed her on. "I will stay here and come with the next load."

"If you are certain?" Bridget hesitated.

"I can tie a bandage and give a drink of water as well as the rest of them."

"Thank you," Bridget mouthed as she climbed onto the bench next to the driver.

"The doctor knew you would be here," the driver said. "He said you would know what to do."

"I hope so," she said with a half smile.

"How bad is it?" she asked.

"It is an awful mess—and that is saying something, 'cause I've been serving since I was of age." He was a burly sergeant of about thirty-five or forty years. "It is muddy, as you would expect after the hard rains, but between the fog and the smoke 'tis impossible to see. The losses are heavy after only a few hours and I hear the Prussians have not arrived yet."

It was slow going through the streets as local people had come out to help and many of the wounded were littered through the streets, too exhausted—or in shock—to go on. Bridget had never seen anything quite like it. She could only imagine what the battlefield must be like. The medical tents must surely be overflowing, for the doctors would have kept those patients too severe to be moved and those they could help. There would be many more loads of injured before the day was done, she knew.

"Have any particular battalions suffered heavy losses?"

"Aye. Picton's Division. General Picton was shot dead on his horse."

Bridget swallowed hard. "Have you seen the 1st Battalion, by any chance?"

"Oh, you have family with them? I see. No, I cannot say as I have seen them."

She nodded. "My father." Bridget glanced at the men who were laid out in the back of the cart.

"What of these poor souls?"

"The sawbones had to amputate a limb on each of them. He said they might have a chance if they survived the infections, and you would give them the attention he could not. I tell you, miss, there have not been many we could save today."

"I pray our fortunes turn quickly." She shivered at the thought. They arrived at the house her father had leased and the servants came out to help her and the sergeant move the men inside. Beds had been made up ready in the drawing room. Thankfully, the servants were amenable to helping her.

Each patient was given a sponge bath and made as comfortable as possible with water to drink and medicine for the pain when necessary. There was little else she could do for them until the fevers began. She very much doubted infection could be avoided, given the condition of the men, for it would take more than a good soaking to remove all of the mud, blood and smoke from them.

Lady Amelia arrived not much later with another cart full of patients and a couple of assistants who were also military wives.

"I brought some more help with me. I hope you do not mind."

"Not at all. I hope you are taking care of yourself," Bridget remembered to remind her. They were both dirty and bloody. Bridget knew she had scarcely stopped to think of herself, and Lady Amelia was not used to this.

"Have you received any word?" Bridget asked, purposely keeping the question vague.

"I saw Lieutenant O'Neill not long after you left the gate and he said it is unbelievably horrid. He said it is not a sure thing at all. If the reinforcements do not arrive, he does not know what will happen."

Bridget felt a tightness in her throat which she could not afford to give into. She knew that it could well be a couple of days before she saw her father and brother again. She could not fret. At least Lieutenant O'Neill had been whole not long ago.

The battle still raged on as she could hear the guns booming in the distance. Lifting her chin, she determined to continue to fight for these poor souls as if they were her own father or brother... or heart.

CHAPTER 5

Tobin had never seen anything like this. He had thought nothing could be worse than Badajoz, but the carnage was unfathomable. When there was an occasional break in the fog and smoke, all that could be seen were thousands upon thousands of human bodies and horses, lying mangled atop each other in mud and blood. It was hard not to be out there fighting, to watch his brethren struggle while he rode in and out with messages from general to general.

Then, when it appeared there was nowhere left to fight, another charge would come over what looked to be impossible terrain. Late in the afternoon there was a break in the fighting and it seemed impossible to go on. It was sweltering in the heat and humidity, and almost unmanageable to breathe with the thick smoke from the cannon and the fires scorching his throat. The sun was already far into the west, and no one wanted to retreat and fight another day.

Tobin did not know how much longer their forces could last. They were decimated. They were hindered by the soft, wet ground, and the passage over the sunken roads littered with dead and wounded was becoming impassable. The cavalry was used up and most of the artillery was in bad shape, but they could not quit now. He rode on towards the east, hoping to receive news that reinforcements had come. A Prussian officer met him beyond the eastern front of the battle and passed over a dispatch, expressing urgency.

Finally, Tobin had a dispatch to run to Wellington that the Prussians were arriving. "Thank God," he whispered, knowing that without the reinforcements, they would not win. He passed the 1st battalion and saw Miss Murphy's father. The general hailed Tobin and asked for a report.

"I hope you have good news, Lieutenant," he said.

"The Prussians have arrived at last," Tobin replied, knowing he had been singled out by the general, but also conscious he was unable to stop for long.

"Thank God. We are about to make a charge to recapture La Haye Sainte," he said to Tobin. "Please give Bridget my love."

Tobin gave a nod and tipped his hat to the general. He must have known his fate, for moments after Tobin rode away, the battalion appeared to be ambushed by cannon fire. Later, it was said they fought dead in a square, but they had held their ground. Only one officer survived, and he was not General Murphy.

Tobin rode on to find Wellington in the thick of the fight, as usual, encouraging his troops to rally for a final stand.

Tobin delivered the long-awaited news, and Wellington sent him on to spread the word to the other commanders so they could rouse the troops for one more push. The cavalry was making a charge to recapture the farm in support of the battalion General Murphy was leading. Tobin saw his former brethren James and Colin and spoke to them quickly before they received the signal to go.

"Thackeray took a bullet in the leg. He was taken to the sawbones," James said.

"I will see if I can find him. The Prussians are here now, so, Lord willing, this will be over soon," Tobin told them.

"Thank God. I do not know how much more we can take," Colin said as they spurred their horses forward.

Tobin watched them go, wishing he were with them, and then rode west towards Château Hougoumont. On the way, he met up with

Captain Murphy, who was passing in the opposite direction with his own reports to the commander.

He was about to return to Wellington when cannon shot exploded a few feet away. The blast threw him from his horse, its shrill neigh of fear ringing in his ears. He hit the ground hard, flat on his back, and in the same instant, Captain Murphy landed on top of him. The shock of the pain and weight winded him. Stunned, he lay there, dragging in stertorous breaths until his lungs eased. He wiggled his fingers and toes, and despite a searing pain in his head, realized he was alive and intact.

Murphy was a dead weight on top of him. "Murphy?"

No response.

"Murphy!" Tobin shouted.

There was still no response. Tobin felt Murphy's head and neck, trying to find some sign of life. A sticky substance oozed out of the base of his neck onto Tobin's glove.

"Oh, please, God, no. No!" Tobin shouted, rolling his comrade off him. He could not tell if he was done for yet, but he would be soon without help.

Tobin scrambled to his feet, looking around for the horses. Murphy's horse was lying not far from where they had landed, writhing and screaming. The gelding had taken more of the shell than Murphy and Tobin had. He walked over to see if there was any hope, but the animal's entire side had been ripped open.

"Ye poor beast." Tobin felt his throat swell, knowing he must put the charger out of his misery. It hurt as much to see a horse fall as it did a human. He lifted his pistol, hand shaking, but gritted his teeth and pulled the trigger. "Forgive me, sir."

He had to attend to Murphy without delay. Such was war. A soldier must go on.

Trojan had shied in the way of his kind, but was well enough trained to the rigours of battle not to have fled and stood, trembling, not twenty feet away. Tobin called Trojan to him and, spying another soldier nearby, summoned the man to help him with Captain Murphy. Tobin did his best to put pressure on the wound and bandage

Murphy's head with the medicaments he carried in his saddle-bags. With the soldier's help, Tobin half lifted, half pushed the captain across Trojan's saddle and then clambered up behind, holding the reins in one hand and clutching his comrade with the other.

Once he was mounted, although vaguely aware of the pains in his own body, he ignored them. Nothing was about to prevent Tobin doing his damnedest to save Murphy.

He directed Trojan to the nearest medical tent, but the sawbones took one look at Murphy's wound and shook his head.

"There is naught I can do to save him, Lieutenant. I must help the ones who have a chance."

Tobin knew he could not leave his friend to die alone. He could never forgive himself. Bridget would never forgive him.

Tobin could not find a wagon to transport his friend, yet neither could he leave Murphy slung over the back of his horse. He again mounted behind the fallen man and began the arduous trek back to Brussels. It was the longest ten miles of his life. He might not be able to save Murphy, but at least he could save him from dying alone and being buried in a mass grave. And, miracles could happen—not that Tobin had ever seen any, nor expected to after this day.

They passed hundreds of soldiers trying to make their way back to Brussels. Bodies littered the road all the way to the gate of the city. Murphy had not regained consciousness and Tobin himself was beginning to feel weak. He was aware of pain in places he had not realized before due to the rush of trying to save Murphy. When he pulled Trojan to a halt in front of the house on the Rue de Loi, Tobin nearly fainted with relief when Miss Murphy and Lady Amelia rushed out to help him.

"We made it here, then," he said to her, even though he was not sure they had at all.

"Yes, Lieutenant O'Neill, you made it here. We have you now."

Servants took over and carried Captain Murphy into one of the rooms in the house. He stood by as he watched sister tend to brother with amazing stoicism. Most ladies would have swooned on the street outside.

Apparently, Murphy had survived the ride back to town. Miss Murphy had re-bandaged his head and was watching him lying in the bed. She looked helpless and Tobin wanted to comfort her, but knew he must return to his duty. He walked forward and placed a hand on her shoulder.

"I must return now."

She turned to look at him, huge tears pooling in her eyes. "But you are wounded!" she said, as though she had just seen him.

"'Tis nothing that cannot be seen to later, lass."

She looked him over, eyes wide. "What happened?"

"A cannon ball hit a few feet away from us and knocked us off our mounts. I probably have a few pieces in me you may dig out later," he said, forcing a half smile.

"You must let me attend to some of those now. Wellington will understand."

Tobin submitted to her ministrations, knowing she needed to do this for him.

Using her surgical tools, she pulled out three large pieces of shrapnel from his leg and one from his head he had not known he had been hit with. She then cleansed each area with strong spirits causing him to curse loudly in Gaelic, but of course, she knew what he was saying and only clicked her tongue at him. She stitched him up and re-bandaged his wounds.

"I cannot convince you to stay?" She stared up at him and his heart ached for her.

"I would if I could, *mo álainn*."

"Thank you for bringing him to me."

Tobin did not have the heart to tell her about her father yet. What a severe blow the loss of both her family members would be to her.

He bent his head and kissed her on the cheek. "I will return when I can."

"I consider that a promise," she whispered.

Tobin found Trojan and remounted as the sun was beginning to fall, ignoring the searing pain in his head. He rode through the forest to the battlefield, praying the surge of the Prussians would be enough. The alternative was unthinkable.

WHEN LIEUTENANT O'NEILL had not come back, Bridget fretted. Why? What could have kept him from fulfilling his promise? *Please, God, let him not have been hurt again or be suffering from the injuries he had already sustained.* She glanced at the bracket clock above the fireplace. It was after midnight; he probably would not come that night now.

She looked at her brother lying on the bed, still unconscious and barely alive. Bridget knew in her heart that the chances of Patrick's recovery were almost nil but she would not give up on him. It was a miracle he was not already dead. If Lieutenant O'Neill had not been there when it happened, he would have died on the battlefield.

The house was already packed with wounded men, as was the one next door. Every bed, sofa, chair and available space on the floor was covered with ailing soldiers. Many of them would not see daylight again, but Bridget would not let them die alone. She would hold their hands and speak loving words to them as they passed on to the afterlife. The first day following a battle was always the hardest. Thankfully, she had a few people to help her so they could take turns to rest. She also needed the male servants' brawn to help change the men who could not see to themselves.

If only she had some news! Perhaps she could slip next door, once she had made the rounds again and ensured everyone was comfortable or as comfortable as it was in her power to make them. Thank God the Duke of Waverley had helped gather supplies and medicaments, or she never would have had enough. Even in her worst nightmares, she could not have foreseen this carnage and she knew the patients she had were only a fraction of what must be innumerable loss. Every house from here to Waterloo was probably full of wounded.

She kissed Patrick on the forehead and went to check how

everyone else did. Most of what could be done had been done and the patients were resting, if restlessly. Two of the helpers were nodding off in chairs, for which Bridget was grateful. There had been hours and hours of tireless work that day.

As she checked two of the more severe cases that had been brought to her by the field doctor, she found they had already passed away. Bridget closed their eyes and said a prayer for them. She would have their bodies laid out in the morning. There would probably be more.

Three soldiers were awake and groaning in pain, so Bridget dosed them with laudanum and made them as comfortable as possible.

When everyone was in as good an order as she could make them, she slipped out of the house to see how Amelia was faring.

The entrance door of the Waverley house was unlocked, and Bridget saw there were as many men quartered there as in her own house, the stench and groans of pain the same. She walked through the rooms, soothing them as she had just done next door. When she went upstairs, she found Amelia with Captain Elliot. Thank God he appeared to be unharmed.

"Forgive my intrusion," Bridget said. "I wanted to see if you needed anything, or required any assistance."

Captain Elliot looked at her with pain in his eyes, as though he had been to Hell and back. He probably had.

"Napoleon is defeated," he replied, "though at a very high price."

"Thank God it is over at least. Are you injured?" she asked him.

"Only a few scratches."

"He feels guilty," Amelia explained.

"So many men died. I have lost another one of my friends, too." He choked on his evident grief and pressed his lips together.

Bridget's heart skipped a beat and it must have shown on her face.

"Colin," he said with difficulty. "He was shot right off his horse in front of me. Just like Peter was." He shook his head. "And Thackeray took a bullet in the leg. He is in the room next door. I have not yet seen James."

"Lieutenant O'Neill?" she ventured. "Have you seen him? My

brother is next door but I doubt he will survive. I have heard nothing of my father, either."

"Oh, Bridget," Amelia said, wrapping her arms around her. Bridget had remained calm so far, but could not prevent a few sobs escaping. When she had composed herself somewhat, Captain Elliot spoke again.

"When last I saw Tobin, he was searching the battlefield. He could be there for days. There were already looters out there." Captain Elliot shook his head. "I must go back, but I wanted to reassure Amelia. I will try to send more help. I know Dr. Wheeler was planning on coming when he could get away."

Bridget let out a sigh of relief. If Lieutenant O'Neill had been searching after the battle was over, at least he must be well enough for now. He would doubtless begin to feel the effects of his wounds—and probable infection—soon though, so she hoped he would not stay out all night, stubborn man that he was.

"I will visit Lord Thackeray before I leave. I will let you say your goodbyes in private." Bridget forced a smile as she spoke.

She went into the next chamber and found the patient awake and trembling. "Lord Thackeray? It is Bridget Murphy. I do not know if you remember me. May I check your leg?"

He was looking at her but not really seeing her. He was in shock. She felt his brow and he was already burning with fever. It seemed too soon, but perhaps he had sustained the injury early on. She pulled back the covers and removed the bandage from the wound. It looked as though the surgeon had dug the bullet out, but little else. She would need to clean the wound well if he was to have any chance of survival. She packed the bandages back into the hole, covered him up and went in search of supplies.

"How is he?" Captain Elliott asked, meeting her in the hall on his way out.

"He is already raging with fever and the wound is dirty. I am going to get my surgical tools from next door.

"I will stay and help you then. You might need me to hold him."

She nodded. "Thank you."

When she came back, Amelia and Captain Elliot were with Lord Thackeray. Amelia was bathing his forehead with damp cloths. Thackeray still wore that blank stare, his gaze centred somewhere over Amelia's shoulder.

"Ready?" Bridget asked.

Captain Elliott gave her a sceptical look. She handed him a bottle of fine brandy. "Give him a good dose of this."

While he poured some of the contents down the patient's throat, she removed the packing she had put into the hole and began cleaning it as best she could, shaking her head at the lack of cleanliness. It was full of debris and pieces of the bullet which had splintered when it hit the bone. This man would be lucky if he did not lose his entire leg, she reflected, but she would do her best to prevent it.

After rinsing the area thoroughly and picking out all the pieces of shot she could see, she spoke to Captain Elliot and Amelia.

"You had better hold his upper body, Captain, and if you can, hold his legs, Amelia. He will not like this no matter how dazed he is."

Slowly, she poured half of the bottle of brandy into the wound.

He roused from the stupor he was in with a string of colourful, choice words and fought Bridget, Amelia and Captain Elliot as though he were back on the battlefield. Snatching one arm free of Captain Elliot's grasp, he flailed wildly and almost pushed Amelia across the room.

"Easy, brother. It is Philip and Miss Murphy. We are trying to save your leg."

He was staring at Captain Elliot and as that gentleman spoke soothing words to him, Lord Thackeray seemed to recognize the voice and settled. His brow was covered in sweat and he began to tremble again.

"You are safe now. 'Tis over. It is all over now," Philip whispered.

Lord Thackeray swallowed and nodded his head. Bridget continued to work on the wound while Captain Elliot and Lady Amelia tried to soothe and calm their friend.

Suddenly, what had happened clearly came back to him and

Bridget almost lost her practised imperturbation when he broke down in tears. She assumed he was remembering that Colin had died.

"Colin!" he wailed and Captain Elliot hugged him hard and wept with him. Bridget and Amelia met each other's gaze and had to turn away. Bridget knew if she gave in to emotion now, she might not stop crying for days.

She stitched what she could of the damaged flesh and re-bandaged the wound. "I must look in on my brother. I will return in a couple of hours to see how Lord Thackeray is doing. If his fever rises, give him some willow bark tea."

Lady Amelia nodded, still unable to speak as the men wept.

Bridget escaped before giving way to her own grief. She could not afford to cry in front of the men. Where, oh where, were her father and Lieutenant O'Neill?

When she returned to see how Patrick was, one look told her all she needed to know. His breathing had deteriorated into gasps. It would not be long now. She curled up on the bed next to him and held him until the end.

CHAPTER 6

*T*obin took a moment to rest against a tree. He had been searching for hours and refused to quit the battlefield. He would not allow someone else to find his friends first or dump them in a mass grave. He knew the cavalry had made a final charge at the same time as General Murphy's battalion. It had been near the farm. They had to be there somewhere. The sight and smell and overwhelming carnality had caused Tobin to retch several times that night.

"Tobin." He heard Philip's voice call to him and looked up through his haze of pain.

Philip dismounted and tied his horse next to Trojan. He handed him a fresh canteen and Tobin took it and drew on it with appreciation. "Are you a mirage?"

"Hardly that. I am all too real. Are you looking for Colin?"

Tobin choked, too tired to hide his emotion. He nodded. "And General Murphy."

"Does she know?" Philip asked.

"I could not bear to tell her. I left her brother there to die. I thought the least I could do was find his body for her."

"What happened to your head?" Philip asked as the first grey of dawn was beginning to breach the sky.

"The same cannon ball that hit Captain Murphy. We were together."

Philip looked away. They were both seasoned soldiers, but the aftermath was always untenable. You always lost someone you knew. Murphy had been on staff with them—it did not take long to get close.

"What of the rest?"

"Thackeray is at the house, delirious from a gun shot wound to his left thigh. Miss Murphy had to clean it out, and I stayed to help. I have not heard from James, but if he was unharmed he would have followed on after the French."

Tobin nodded.

"Where have you looked?"

"Only this side of the farm from there to this tree. It is hard work lifting the bodies and horses. I've had to threaten many of the looters with violence. *Gommeril gobshites.*"

"I do not know how you have gone at it alone, and with the look of your head 'tis a wonder you are still standing."

Tobin did not want to think about his head. It was being a nuisance, for it was pounding like a hammer from the inside.

"Both of them should be in this vicinity. It was the last I saw of them. I wanted to be methodical. It would be too easy to miss them." Tobin did not need to explain, he knew. Many of the bodies were destroyed or mangled beyond recognition. He might never find them, but he would continue to search until he could go on no more.

"You are sure their men did not recover them?"

"I am sure of nothing. But I was afraid not to look. I heard only one officer survived from the 27th."

"Then we shall continue." Philip took a pistol from his saddle-bag and holstered it. It was coming on to daylight, but those who robbed the poor soldiers' bodies had been known to be violent. They were not the only ones out looking. Wails of horror and cries of despair echoed through the valley as more people joined the search. Hell could be no worse than this. Tobin would never be able to forget.

"There have to be twenty thousand dead out here, at least," Philip remarked as they began to move body after body to see if it was a friend or dear one. Two hours later, after making a circuit of La Haye Sainte, they finally found General Murphy buried in his square underneath the red uniforms of his men, the look on his face one that would never leave Tobin's memories.

"They really were ambushed by the cannon," Philip said as they both barely held back their bile. "I will fetch the horses."

Tobin ran over to a rare patch of grass to vomit again as soon as Philip had passed behind the building. One never got used to this part —so full of life one moment, and inert the next.

Give my love to Bridget.

He could still hear the pain in the general's voice echoing through the valley. How was he to tell her? How could he help her?

I would like to know someone would look after my sister should some-thing happen to my father and me. There is only an elderly aunt and she is not someone you would choose to know willingly. He could hear Patrick's voice saying the words to him.

Philip returned with the horses and they managed to place the general's body on top of Trojan, who shied a bit at the smell, but calmed when Tobin told him quietly to stand.

"Every one of these men deserves a proper burial," Tobin said achingly, knowing most would end up in unmarked, mass graves, here on the field of battle.

There was no response from his companion.

"Colin must have gone further," Philip said, looking out over the valley.

"I have not crossed the road."

"Hopefully, there is not too much farther to go."

It took them another hour to find Colin, and Philip dropped to his knees and wept openly. Quiet, steady, conservative Colin; the haunted last look on his face as he realized his fate.

His horse had fallen with him and they had to pull his body out from under the dead beast. By the time they pried his body out, the sun was already warm in the sky. You would never have known by looking up at the peaceful heavens how Hell's bowels had opened the day before to enact one of its scenes on this valley. No doubt Satan had a hand in yesterday's work.

The men began the slow walk back to Brussels, leading the horses. Neither spoke a word the entire way, even though at times Tobin did not know if he would reach the Flemish capital. Now that his self-imposed commission had been completed, he could feel every place he had been hit.

It felt like a funeral procession along the road as the people looking for kith and kin, and some of those who had been called to bury the dead, would stop and bow heads or salute as they passed. It would take days, if not weeks, to bury what amounted to a small city of dead. Bodies were scattered along the road back to Brussels, many those who had survived the battlefield only to die on their way to seek help. There had to be as many on the French side as well.

Tobin was dirty and dizzy, and felt as though he would die of thirst. He experienced again the sensation of being in a tunnel. At least walking through the forest provided some shade, a slight reprieve from the sun's heat.

By the time they halted the horses in front of the two houses, Tobin was seeing double and could barely put one foot in front of the other. Miss Murphy and Lady Amelia must have been watching for them for Miss Murphy rushed out to him. He was aware of uttering the words, "I am sorry," before he surrendered to his own injuries and collapsed to the pavement at her feet.

"YOU STUPID MAN!" Bridget said, exasperated with Lieutenant O'Neill as he fell at her feet. She barely caught his head before it hit the pavement.

"Help me get him inside!" Bridget called to Captain Elliot, who had been greeting his wife and had not seen O'Neill fall.

"Tobin!" Captain Elliot shouted, immediately running over to help.

Two of the servants must have heard the commotion, for they came hurrying down the steps.

Bridget directed them to her bedchamber; it was the only place left to put him.

"Why, you idiotic man?" she asked him as she began to strip away his uniform. It was covered with mud and blood. "He needs water," she said to Amelia, who was standing a few feet away, waiting to help.

"He would not stop until he found them both," Captain Elliott said softly. "I confess, I did not realize how badly he was hurt. He must have suffered dreadfully on the walk back. The day was sweltering."

Bridget's eyes filled with tears. She knew he had done this for her. That had been her father's body lying across his horse... but she could do no more for her father and she still had the chance to save Tobin—Lieutenant O'Neill.

"Help me undress him and bathe him," she said briskly to cover her feelings. "I want to look at his head. It was the most severe of the injuries he had sustained when I saw him yesterday."

All three of them worked on Tobin for some time. Amelia tried to hydrate the man—in small amounts so he would not choke—after Philip had helped her to change and bathe him. Meanwhile, Bridget doctored the various wounds, two of which Tobin had pulled open during his search through the night.

"You foolish man," she muttered at least a hundred times. Yet, he was already so very dear. She could not lose him, too. At that moment, she would have given anything for those green eyes to open and for him to make some cheeky remark to her, but she knew it would be some considerable time before that happened, if at all. He had exhausted himself and he would become feverish. It was inevitable.

The three of them had done all they could for the moment. Walking out into the hall, Captain Elliot leaned negligently against the wall while Bridget and Amelia perched against the banister. No one wanted to speak of her father and brother, Bridget knew. Nevertheless, she could not ignore the fact they must be dealt with soon. The death-cart had, that morning, taken away the six men they had lost, between the two houses, during the night.

Bridget had maintained her composure fairly well, considering. Once everyone was gone, the knowledge of her loss would hit her hard, but for now she had to stay strong for those people who still had a chance of living.

"I do not know what to do," she said quietly.

"We will take care of you, Bridget," Amelia answered.

"It is not so much myself I worry about. Father said he had provided for me. I do not know how to bury them here. I cannot fathom trying to return to Ireland with their bodies."

"Is that what you wish to do?" Philip asked.

"I do not know," she whispered. "Is it possible? I think my father would want that. My mother is buried there."

"I can try to make arrangements, but it must be done quickly. There are others who will be returned for burial."

"It seems selfish of me. There are so many here who need my help."

"I will go and discover what arrangements are already being made. You do know it is never expected of you to run a hospital by yourself, do you not? There will be ships taking as many of the wounded back as can be managed. I will see if I can arrange passage for you."

"I will not leave Lieutenant O'Neill behind."

"Tobin is as tough as they come. He is too stubborn to die of something as menial as a wound from shrapnel," Philip teased, trying to lighten the mood. "None of us will leave Tobin behind. The sneaky rogue would not leave me in peace; I will not let him go without equal suffering."

He kissed Amelia on the cheek and took Bridget's hands and looked her in the eye. "I am so very sorry, Bridget. We will help you with this dreadful situation." He dropped a brotherly kiss on her forehead and hurried down the stairs.

Amelia wrapped her arms around Bridget and somehow they slid to the floor, sobbing in each other's arms.

"Thank you. I feel better now," Bridget said, wiping away the remnants of her much needed cry. "I must go and look in on Lord Thackeray. Take a few minutes to rest. There is a truckle bed in my bedroom and you will be there if Tobin awakes."

"I will agree to rest if you promise you will do the same when I wake up." Amelia sighed.

"I do not think my body will allow me to do otherwise," Bridget said with a reluctant smile. She had not slept for more than a few minutes here and there in the last two days. There should be no more influx, and hopefully, the patients would be stable enough over the next day or two that the nursing shifts could be rotated a little better. If she was to leave for Ireland, though, arrangements would have to be made for all the soldiers. For now, she was too tired to worry or even grieve properly. She walked next door to see how Lord Thackeray was healing. He had been in the depths of a fever when she left him last. When she entered the room, she found the doctor was with him.

"Good afternoon, lass. I saw them bring your father in. I am so very sorry." He had already seen Patrick's body. "They were both very fine men."

"Thank you," she replied softly.

"Do you know what you will do?"

"Captain Elliott is trying to make arrangements. If possible, I will take them to Ireland to bury them beside my mother."

"If you need anything, you need only ask—including a home. It will not be the same if you are not my best assistant."

Bridget forced a smile. It was true; she knew no other life and Dr. Wheeler had always been kind to her. She would have to marry him to stay, and she just could not imagine being wed to someone who was more of a father figure.

"I do not know what I will do yet. It will take some time to make arrangements."

"The offer always stands, lass, though I know I am not much to offer. A pretty lady like you could have anyone she wanted."

"You are very kind." She reached over and touched his hand. "Now, how is my lord doing?"

"You did a good job cleaning his wound. It looks as well as can be expected. The fever is in his blood and it is now up to him to fight it."

"Lieutenant O'Neill is next door. Would you have a look at him? He was hit by the same cannon shot as Patrick, but did not bear the brunt of it. I pulled four pieces of shrapnel out of his leg and head and cleaned him up, but the idiotic man went out searching for my father and a friend. He was out all night. He collapsed at my feet earlier today, in front of the house."

"Idiotic indeed." He shook his head. "Loyalty and honour. They put it above good sense."

They walked back to her house and she followed him up to where Tobin was resting. Amelia was resting on the bed nearby. Bridget stood at the door while the doctor examined Tobin.

He came back out into the hall and spoke to her quietly, though Bridget was sure nothing shy of a cannon shot would wake either of them at this point.

"He needs rest and water more than anything just now. He will probably have to fight the fevers. You know all this, lass. You just wanted reassurance?"

"I want to know if he is strong enough to make the trip back to Ireland."

He looked her in the eye and seemed to understand. "If he has you to care for him, he will do as well on a boat as in this bed."

"I cannot leave him here," she explained. "He brought Patrick and father back to me. I owe him that much, at least."

"Do not do it out of debt alone, lass. That is a life sentence if not done for the right reasons."

"I know it, and I appreciate your concern. I believe it is the right thing to do. I hope he wakes up before I have to make the decision alone."

The doctor took his leave and Bridget peered back into the room where Tobin was seemingly sleeping peacefully on the bed. She knew he would take care of her out of honour, but was it what he wanted?

Bridget wrestled with what to do. If only he would wake up.

CHAPTER 7

*W*ellington stood beside Tobin's bedside several minutes. "I have lost too many friends in this bad business. I was growing fond of O'Neill. He had best recover."

Tobin heard familiar voices in the distance, and he felt as if he were in a dream he could not wake from. He was so tired but he was drawn to the voices from the depths of somewhere far away.

"He has the best nurse there is." Captain Elliot's tone was reassuring.

"Yes, Miss Murphy. That is a rotten situation; both were damned fine soldiers. What will she do?" Wellington asked.

"She asked me to arrange for the bodies to be sent to Ireland. I assume she means to accompany them," Captain Elliot replied.

"Alone?" Wellington asked with his disapproving voice.

"I have not yet asked her. I assume that, at the very least, her maid will accompany her. Amelia and I are to go to Paris with you."

"I do not like it," the Duke stated.

"Nor I, but it is unfortunately what happens some times."

"See to it that she has what she needs, and send O'Neill home for convalescence."

"Yes, sir. I am already working on it."

"Good, good. I plan to head to Paris on the morrow."

"We will be ready."

"Ah, Miss Murphy. May I offer my deepest sympathies? I cannot say how troubled I am by your losses," Wellington said.

"Thank you, your Grace. They both died for something they believed in. Thank God we won, so their loss is not in vain." *The voice of an angel*, Tobin thought drowsily.

"By God, I hope not. We will miss having you to help us. My door is always open if you have need of me."

Wellington took his leave, and Tobin drifted in and out of his senses. Not many minutes later, however, there was more commotion to drag him from the fog.

"Waverley. What are you doing back here?" Captain Elliot asked, his voice lifting in surprise.

"We had not yet crossed the Channel when I heard the news. I came back to see if I was needed."

"By Jove, yes. I must follow on to Paris, and I was loath to send Thackeray and O'Neill back to England on a packet in their condition, and Colin's parents would want his body returned."

The room was silent for some moments, until the sound of a nose blowing into a handkerchief cut through the heavy stillness.

"I am sorry. I assumed you had been told."

"I should not be surprised, but it never grows any easier to hear such tidings," the Duke said. He was clearly still deeply affected by the news.

"No," Captain Elliot agreed solemnly.

"How is Tobin?"

"He has been asleep since yesterday. I am hoping he will awake soon. Instead of having his injuries attended to, he exhausted himself to recover Colin and General Murphy."

"That sounds like Tobin," Waverley replied.

"How soon can they be moved?"

"The doctor said he saw no harm in transporting them now. I was hoping Lieutenant O'Neill would awaken first," Miss Murphy said.

"Perhaps he still will, Bridget." That was Lady Amelia's voice.

Tobin was trying to wake up. Truly he was. *Bridget. Yes. Mo álainn.* Could she not hear him?

"He is growing restless. Perhaps we should let him rest," she said.

"We can discuss our plans in another room," Waverley answered.

No! Do not leave! I am trying to talk to you.

"Shh. Calm yourself," she said in a soothing voice. "I want you to wake up, but calmly." A cool cloth greeted his forehead, followed by a glass of water being pressed to his lips, which he drank greedily. He was so very thirsty.

"That gives me hope. It is the first time you have drunk more than a sip."

He would do that and much more if she wanted him to. *Just don't leave me.* The mattress sagged as she sat on the side of the bed, and he was filled with her warmth and scent of gardenias.

"I wish you were awake to talk to. You were a good listener, and I do not know what to do."

He was trying. Why could he not wake up? He could hear her.

"You see, I think I should take Father and Patrick back to Ireland." She inhaled a ragged breath. "I was hoping you would go with me." Her throat sounded thick with tears. "I do not want to go alone."

I would go anywhere for you.

"I know it is scandalous to wish it or ask it of you. I know you would feel obligated to protect me. And now the Duke has come to take you home. I should let you go."

Home. He had no home.

"And I cannot take you with me when you are unconscious. I have no right to you, Tobin. I wish we had had more time together before the war." She uttered a harsh laugh. "It is how life seems to work, though. You find happiness within reach only to have it snatched out of your grasp."

Tobin.

A light knock on the door interrupted their conversation.

"Doctor Wheeler. How are you today?" she asked, rising from the bed. Tobin was not happy about her leaving his side. He tried to reach for her, but his hands would not cooperate.

"There have been too many losses, lass, for my peace of mind. How is the patient today? I was informed he will be leaving tomorrow, along with Lord Thackeray."

And Bridget. He could not leave her.

"I thought he was trying to wake up, a few minutes ago. He grew agitated, but settled again after some water and the application of cool cloths."

Tobin felt large hands examining him. They were not soothing like hers. The doctor was unwinding his bandages and causing unnecessary pain. Tobin groaned.

"He is responding to pain. That is good," the evil man said. "These wounds look to be healing well."

Suddenly, the man's hands were prying his eyes open, and Tobin wished his body would cooperate. He could not see anything, but a bright sensation sent a fiery pain throughout his head. He wished the man to the *divil.*

"Perhaps, when the swelling on his brain goes down, he will wake up. He was not rendered unconscious from the blast itself."

"If only it would be today," Miss Murphy added.

"He will recover in his own time—or not. You know how it is."

She sighed. "I do."

"I wish you the best of good wishes, Miss Murphy."

"Perhaps we will meet again, sir. I do hope so."

Footsteps receded from the room, and Tobin felt a hand stroking back the hair on his forehead. He wanted to purr like a cat.

"What am I to do?" she asked in a desperate voice. "I am afraid to go alone. Afraid I will never see you again. I suppose I do not have a choice, do I?" She took his hand in hers and he felt her lips kiss the back of his hand before she set it back on the bed and walked away.

He was going to have to manage to wake up soon, but the pain in his head was too much for now, and he slipped back into oblivion.

Tobin could not wake. He knew he was in the thick of a battle, for the stench was unmistakable—stagnant blood, excrement, smoke... he had to hurry. The men were giving up, but help was coming. He had to tell them as quickly as possible. He urged Trojan forward, searching for the next courier.

Suddenly, the ground shook beneath him and he was flying through the air. The muddy ground softened the blow, but not enough. The wind was knocked out of his lungs and he lay still, struggling to breathe and make sense of where he was. As he slowly came to, he realized something was weighting him down. He forced his eyes open to see the face of Captain Murphy not far from his own. Good God, they had been hit.

Tobin struggled to move, but Murphy was dead weight. Panic set in as he realized he was trapped and his friend lay dead on top of him. Breaking out in a cold sweat, he gasped for air, but he could not breathe and he could not move. He opened his mouth to cry for help, but no sound came out. He could not wake up. He would die here. Would they bury him alive? Again, he opened his mouth to scream, "I'm alive!" But no one could hear him.

~

GRIEF WAS A STRANGE THING. Bridget suddenly felt she needed to escape, as though the walls were closing in on her. She ran down the stairs and then pulled up short in the entrance hall, not even certain there was a horse she could ride.

Captain Elliot was standing just inside the small saloon, speaking with one of the men.

"Miss Murphy? Is something wrong?" he asked.

She shook her head. "No. Yes. My apologies, sir. Yes, I need to go out. Is there a horse I may ride?"

"As far as I know, your horses are still here. Where are you going? Would you like for me to have Amelia accompany you?" He looked worried.

"No, but thank you. I need to be alone for a while."

Captain Elliot nodded. He understood, and the last thing she cared about at the moment was propriety.

She would not be requiring her father's and brother's horses any more, would she? Patrick's favourite horse had died with him, she'd been told. Swallowing hard, she went to the mews and saddled her mare. In the panic before the battle, people had been paying outrageous sums for horses or even stealing them in order to flee the area. By some remarkable circumstance, theirs had been kept safe.

Bridget mounted and headed south with no intentional direction, heedless of possible danger from looters or French deserters. Perhaps, subconsciously, she had an unrecognized urge to see where her father and brother had died. A measure of peace might then be hers.

The Soignes Forest was calm and quiet with a slight breeze rustling through the canopy of trees. Thankfully, there was no sign of the dead and wounded littering the road today.

Bridget continued at a sedate trot, taking in all that was around her. As she reached the edge of the valley where the battle had taken place, she inhaled sharply as a rush of feeling came over her. It was a strange sensation of troubled spirits and she felt overwhelmed. She stopped and listened, closing her eyes the better to hear instead of fighting the sensation. After earlier battles, she had occasionally thought she had seen or heard spirits, but there had been nothing like this. The howling and moaning of death and destruction; the smell of mud and life's blood pouring out the loss of innocence… it was so real she could see it, smell it, taste it. She opened her eyes abruptly to make it stop. What she saw then were soldiers digging and bodies being piled into mass graves, her father's men likely included. She turned away to compose herself. She had seen it before, but it did not stop the pain.

Although it was not her duty to perform, Bridget decided she would write to each family or visit them when she returned home. It was the least she could do, and what her father always did. With a little nod of determination, she rode on.

First, she came to a farm house. This must be La Haye Sainte, where her father and Captain Smith had fallen. She sat atop her horse on the crest overlooking the valley, which was littered with debris and the things that would not be worth money to the looters. All that was valuable was long gone, but there was still enough to attest to the atrocity of the loss of life sustained. *God, let it be worth it*, she whispered. She could envision it: her father's brave infantrymen formed in a square as the French cavalry charged at them.

A tear rolled down her cheek as she manoeuvred the horse down and around the farm house. When she reached the east side, something inside her made her stop and dismount. She walked around, looking at the ground and guessing where they must have died. Pieces of their red wool uniforms, bits of canteen and sword handles remained, dotted among craters in the ground left by cannon balls... Bridget knelt down and picked up a handle which held her family crest.

"Oh, Papa!" she cried, unable to abate the tears as they fell. She stood there for some time, accepting that her father's spirit had left him here. It gave her a small measure of peace as she turned and walked her mare towards the Château Hougoumont. It had been near there that Patrick and Tobin had met their fate. She was unable to find the precise spot where they had been hurt, but she sat near a hole in the ground where a cannon had left its mark. It mattered less because she had been able to say goodbye to Patrick and be with him when he breathed his last. She had his personal effects to keep. For some while she sat still, reconciling herself before standing again to leave. Taking one last look over the valley that had taken her family, she uttered a prayer for their souls' journey to the afterlife, knowing they knew no pain in Heaven. "Goodbye, Father. Goodbye, Patrick."

She found a place to remount her mare and did not look back again, unseeing, through a shower of tears, for most of her return journey to Brussels. It had been necessary to go—she would have always wondered otherwise, she knew, as she clutched the handle belonging to her father's sword tight in her hand.

EARLY THE NEXT MORNING, carriages and wagons arrived to transport all those being treated in the two houses. Those who were well enough would go on with their regiments or on packets back to England, while a few would be placed in hospitals in Brussels. Lady Amelia and Captain Elliot were to go with Wellington on to Paris, and the two houses would be closed. It felt so very final.

Bridget looked out of the window and saw three plain coffins being loaded into a wagon. Bridget still could not believe they were gone. It felt as though they had just not returned from the battle.

"Bridget?" Lady Amelia asked. Bridget turned towards the voice.

"I came to take my leave of you. Will you write to me once you are settled?"

Settled seemed such a foreign word. She could not remember a time when such a word had applied to her.

"Of course. I do not know where that will be."

"I do not like you going alone. Waverley intends to take you with him and make arrangements for you. The Duchess and baby are waiting in Ostend with the boat."

Bridget was a bit stunned. The news was unexpected. "That is very kind of him, but I do not wish to cause him trouble."

"He insists, and so do I, otherwise I would be going with you. Perhaps he does so because he wants your help with Tobin and Thackeray," Amelia added with a twinkle in her eye, though Bridget knew she was trying to make her feel more comfortable.

"That is probably the case," she agreed.

It was also a huge relief to Bridget. She had travelled alone before, of course, but she had never truly been alone in the world. She had no one now.

Amelia held out her arms and Bridget went into them. They had become friends without many words, but would feel close forever with what they had shared. Most ladies would never understand.

Bridget clung harder than she should have done, but when Amelia stepped back, she smiled. "I will see you again soon. I promise. If you ever need any little thing, you may always ask me—or Meg."

"Thank you. Hopefully you will see no more battles."

"I pray not," she said before she left the room. Bridget listened to her boots click across the entrance hall and descend the front steps. Looking out of the window, she saw Captain Elliot and Amelia climb into the carriage and roll away down the street. How she wished things were different and she was going to Paris with them! A tear fell down her cheek and she wiped it away. She would have plenty of time for sorrow later. Today she must help everyone on their way and finish packing her belongings.

The Duke and Captain Elliott had gone to great lengths to arrange things so quickly. Bridget barely had time to check every patient one last time, to make certain they were ready to be transported, before they were all loaded into carriages and leaving her.

Almost before she turned around, Lord Thackeray was being carried downstairs on a makeshift stretcher by two hefty footmen, who must have come with the Duke. Thackeray still looked feverish and Bridget dreaded the carriage ride with him. It would be difficult to keep him, and Tobin, comfortable all the way to the coast.

Each man was to be placed across a bench seat. Bridget looked at Waverley, wondering how he proposed to fit the two of them inside as well. He was probably going to ride.

"Shall I ride on the floor?" she asked, attempting a little humour and yet also a little frightened. "I have endured worse."

"Either that, or we each hold one of their heads—or feet—in our laps," he replied with a hint of sarcasm. "I hope you will not mind my company over that of your maid. We will collect Meg in Ostend for the voyage to England."

"I am most grateful for your assistance, sir." She was also surprised he would be riding with them, if truth be told.

"Would you prefer Thackeray or Tobin?" he asked.

"I'll take the pretty lady, ye daft duke," Tobin answered.

Bridget had never been so happy to hear Irish brogue in her life. Her eyes turned to meet a pair of green ones, as their owner came down the steps with the assistance of the footmen. "About time, ye *leathcheann mór*," she answered back with a strong lilt.

CHAPTER 8

$\mathcal{T}$obin started awake to the presence of two burly, uniformed men—one grabbing his legs, and one his arms. He began to kick and flail, fighting out of instinct. The enemy would not take him alive.

"Sir! Stop fighting!" one said.

"He must think we are the Frogs," another reasoned.

"We mean you no harm, sir. We 'ave come to take you home," one explained.

"Home?" He settled for a moment. Fighting hurt his head.

"Aye. The Duke is here, and Miss Murphy, with a carriage to take you to a ship."

Tobin closed his eyes. *I'm awake! I'm awake*, he rejoiced to himself.

"Can we take you now? Without you fighting, like?"

"I need to wash and dress."

The two footmen looked at each other and shrugged. "His trunk is right there. I don't as see why not," said the one who seemed to be in charge. "As long as you hurry, sir. We can fetch his lordship and come back for you."

Tobin nodded. "I can be quick."

They left him alone and he sighed deeply. *Thank God.* He felt weak, and he ached like the devil, but he was alive and Waverley had come to take him home.

He stood up slowly, his legs shaking, and a flush spread over him. How long had he been lying there? He remembered hearing voices and trying to wake up, but how long had it been? He looked in the glass and his beard told him it had been days. He splashed cold water from the basin on his face and washed quickly. Even that exertion made him feel close to passing out, but it felt good to be clean. Someone must have taken good care of him, though, because he could have smelled much worse.

Tobin rested a moment on a chair before he could summon the effort to get his clothes from the trunk. He lifted the lid to find his uniform laundered and folded neatly on top. He looked at it, noticing that the tears from the shrapnel had been patched and carefully mended. His throat tightened at the memory. He did not want to wear it again, but knew he must. Dressing carefully, he then sat back on the chair to wait, leaning his head against the cushion and closing his eyes against his body's revolt at movement. He desperately wanted to crawl back into bed and sleep for a few more days, but if Waverley and Miss Murphy were waiting for him, then he would not keep them.

Miss Murphy. *Bridget.* She had said many things to him. Did she mean them? Or had it been a dream?

He heard the footmen returning for him and put his hands on the arms of the chair to stand. He would walk to her, by God. She had worried enough about him for a lifetime.

Both of the footmen frowned when they saw him.

"I think we should carry you down, sir. You do not look so good," one of them said.

"I am able to walk. Not very well, I grant you. You may assist me down the stairs so I do not fall."

They went slowly, and his legs shook and he was sweating profusely by the time they reached the front steps, but he had done it.

The Duke and Miss Murphy were standing in front of the carriage, speaking. It was good to see them. It was far better than good.

"Would you prefer Thackeray or Tobin?" Waverley asked Miss Murphy.

"I'll be taking the pretty lady, ye daft duke," Tobin answered.

"Tobin, thank God!" Waverley said at once, and gathered him into a hug, saving him from the disgrace of falling on the pavement again. "The Duchess is cross with you for scaring us so."

A cold sweat was replacing the hot sweat of exertion and Tobin was about to swoon. "I will make it up to her. Can we get in the carriage, now? Otherwise I will be a pancake on the pavement at any second."

"Yes, of course." The Duke released Tobin and helped him climb in.

Thackeray was lying on one of the benches, looking very pale and feverish. Tobin sat on the opposite bench and leaned his head back. He felt as though he had run twenty miles and all he had done was get dressed and walk down the stairs!

The carriage lurched to the side as Miss Murphy and the Duke joined them. It was a luxurious carriage, but this would be no pleasant journey with two invalids and two extra people crowded inside.

"I will sit with Thackeray," Waverley pronounced.

Tobin watched out of half-closed eyes as Miss Murphy nodded and sat next to him.

"You need to lie down, Lieutenant O'Neill. You do not look well," she scolded.

"I do not feel well," he confessed, "but I will not inconvenience you all the way to the coast."

She gave him a stern look which made him want to kiss her.

"I had expected you still to be incapacitated." She took a pillow from the bench beside her and placed it in her lap. "Rest your head here, now," she commanded.

"I would not argue with a beautiful lady," Waverley advised, looking much amused. He was already sitting down with Thackeray's head in his lap.

The carriage lurched forward and Tobin almost retched. Miss Murphy's hands instantly drew his head into her lap and thinking better of his show of pride, he went willingly. It was not long until he was lulled to relaxation by her hands soothing his forehead with gentle motions and cool cloths. She had thought of everything, bless her. He closed his eyes and rested, even though he could hear them speaking.

"It was good of him to wake up," Waverley remarked.

"Yes, indeed. Though I fear he needs more time to heal. I imagine he insisted on dressing and walking down the stairs."

Tobin smiled at the tone in her voice.

"I see your smile, you idiotic man."

"Yes, I heard you call me that a few hundred times over the last few days."

Waverley laughed.

"You could hear?" She sounded exasperated.

"Quite a lot. I do not know if I heard everything or not, but I know you were there."

She was silent as she reached down to pour some water from a jar on the cloth before placing it over his forehead and eyes again.

"I am sorry about your father and brother," he said softly.

"Thank you," she whispered. "We are taking them with us."

He nodded, then winced.

"Keep still."

"How is Thackeray?"

"Still not out of danger," she said quietly in his ear. "He still has fevers and delirium, though his leg is healing nicely. I do not know if he will be able to walk normally or not. One can never tell until a patient makes the attempt."

"How did you know to come back?" he asked the Duke.

"We had not left Ostend because the waters were too unsettled for Meg. News travels fast between the people fleeing Brussels, and I was able to intercept some of the dispatchers while they waited for ships. I did not know details about you or the other brethren, but I heard how bad the battle was. Meg stayed there, but sent me back to find out what I could. She knew I would fret horribly otherwise. I am glad she did."

"Me too."

Not long after they left the gates of the city, they hit a large bump in the road which caused all of them to bounce in their seats. Thackeray began shaking violently, so Miss Murphy had to abandon Tobin to see to him. He wanted her back.

He opened one eye a crack so as to watch her. She helped the Duke subdue Thackeray with more cool cloths and she dosed him with something that calmed him within a few minutes. Her competence impressed him. It was too bad that ladies could not be doctors. She was more skilled than many he had seen in the field.

He closed his eyes after she returned to her seat and once more supported his head. He tried not to think about her in ways he should not, but it was so very lovely to be in her arms with the scent of gardenias and soft woman surrounding him. The pleasant thoughts were quickly replaced by more morose ones. How would he support her if they did marry? Would he be discharged from the army or would he go back? She deserved much more than he could give her. She deserved someone of her own class who could support her in the style to which she was accustomed. It was time for her to have a better life than following the drum—even if that was what she knew and was used to.

Nonetheless, by God and the heavens above, he wanted her. Selfishly, he wanted to steal her away and keep her to himself.

"Why the frown?" she asked as Waverley's soft snores filled the carriage.

"I am worried about you," he answered honestly.

"And I am worried about you," she retorted, bending down to kiss him softly on the forehead.

"Have mercy, lass. I am only human."

His eyes opened into hers. She was watching him with a pleading look.

"Your father and brother would not approve of me as a husband. I have nothing to offer," he said, watching her in his turn.

"I beg to disagree. I am the one with nothing to offer."

"Oh, lass. Ye know I want ye. Who in his right mind would not? But I am not for the likes of ye."

She smiled down at him, making his heart lurch. "Rest for now. We will talk more later."

~

THE CARRIAGE RIDE EVENTUALLY ENDED and they joined the Duchess and daughter at a hotel in Ostend. Soon after, they boarded the ship to England. Time was of the essence, after all, even though Bridget did not like to think about it. The coffins had been placed down in the hull, and she would journey on to Ireland as soon as the others disembarked at Portsmouth. The Duke had argued repeatedly with her and insisted that he accompany her to Ireland.

She had argued in her turn that it was more important for him to take care of the living and return Lord Thackeray to his family. She had assured him her aunt would be there and if his ship took her to Dungarvan, it was then only a short carriage ride to her family's estate. His servants and her maid would be accompanying her, she had reminded him.

Bridget should have buried her brother and father in Belgium. Her father would not have expected her to lay him to rest with her mother, but she felt it was the right thing to do and people did not seem to mind helping her to do it. Perhaps it would afford her a small measure of peace and the time alone would give her some clarity. She was already a spinster and on the shelf, after all.

Bridget stood watching the water as the ship sliced through the sea with its sails catching the wind. It was fascinating to behold and she was lost, mostly alone, to her thoughts. Tobin and Lord Thackeray had been settled to rest on bunks in the cabins, and the Duke and Duchess discreetly left her to her reflections. Now that the journey was almost ended, she had to face what was ahead.

She had no idea how her father had provided for her. They had always been comfortable and she had a modest dowry. Would it be enough to live on? She wondered if she could start some kind of school to teach women to nurse. It would be considered outrageous and most likely would require more funds than she would have. It was a thought. She doubted she would have enough funds to live independently, but she did not rightly know. And what of Tobin? He had put off her suggestions to marry. She had been silly to think he might wish to return to Ireland with her. Had he not said he had escaped from there? She was the daft fool to have thought it.

Too soon, land was coming into view. She was not ready to say goodbye and be alone. Bridget turned back from her perch along the railing to see the Duke and Duchess speaking with Tobin. They had been giving her privacy, she supposed. She smiled at the sight of Tobin. Even with a bandage around his head he was a handsome devil.

He said something to the Duke and Duchess before holding onto the railing and walking slowly towards her. She waited for him.

His smile warmed her insides.

"You are looking improved," she said, trying to be more cheerful than she felt.

"I imagine I could hardly look worse than I did when I fell at your feet. I do not want to know how much you had to do for me. I know I am in your debt."

She shook her head. "If you had not returned Patrick and Father to me you would not have needed my help." She gave him a scolding look, which he ignored.

"What is this I hear of you travelling to Ireland alone?" His gaze bore straight through her.

"You did return them to me for a proper burial, did you not?"

"Aye, but that is not what I meant and you know it, lass. Did you not mean the things you said to me when you thought I could not hear?"

Bridget's breath caught and she looked away as the wind whipped her hair in her face. She did not bother to move it away.

"You should not take anything I said seriously. It was said under duress. I will do very well, Tobin."

"I am sure you will. You are a remarkable woman, but I will at least see you safe to your home."

"No. I will not ask it of you. I have since remembered what you said about Ireland and making your escape."

Tobin leaned over the railing and did not speak for several minutes. She stood with her back against it and waited.

"It is true I never thought to go back, but I promised your brother and your da. The last thing he said to me was, *Give my love to Bridget*. And Patrick made me promise I would look after you." He turned his head towards her with tears in his eyes.

Bridget was unsure what to say. She had not expected this kind of emotion from him, and she knew how much a promise meant to a gentleman. Yet not once had he spoken about doing it for her or because he wanted to, nor had he indicated he returned her affection. She knew he cared for her as a friend, but kisses did not mean promises to men.

"I appreciate you telling me that. It is somehow comforting to know they were thinking of me, but I am not your responsibility, Tobin. You may consider whatever promise you made to them fulfilled."

"I will not let you go alone, lass," he said. "I will follow you until I know you are settled."

"It would not be proper," she said.

"Proper can go hang. You have lost your father and brother and you need to see them buried." His jaw clenched and his fists were balled as he looked out at the approaching shoreline. How she wished they could go back to the happy times: walking in the park and waltzing at a ball; laughing at the ridiculous and preposterous. Would she ever be happy again?

"You need to go home and heal. The Duke has made arrangements for me from here to my home. I will be well enough." It was not what she wished to say. She wanted to scream, 'yes, come with me!', except she had no right.

"I cannot offer you what you deserve, lass," he said, as if reading her thoughts.

"And what is that?" she asked, still wanting to scream. "A knight on a horse riding to my rescue and carrying me away to a big castle?"

"You at least deserve a gentleman who can support you," he answered, insufferably calm while she was raging inside.

"I forget. You are no gentleman. You think I need a big house and fancy clothes. I would have thought you knew me better than that. If you do not wish to marry me, then we will part now. I cannot bear it any more."

She walked away as he reached for her. "Lass, no."

Without a word or a glance, she kept going.

If only they had had more time together before this happened, but friendship and two kisses was not enough reason for her to expect him to take on the responsibility of a wife when he clearly did not wish to do so.

She crossed the deck to say goodbye to the Duchess while the crew eased the ship into the docks. As soon as everything was unloaded, they would set sail again.

Bridget was in low spirits as she spoke her farewells to the Duke and Duchess, and her farewell with Tobin hurt as acutely as her father's and brother's deaths did. Why was that? Perhaps because he was still alive and she had hoped... foolishly, she had hoped. Where was he? She wanted to see him leave and be alone. Would he take his leave or accept her words as the final parting?

She watched as one coffin was loaded with some trunks into a wagon, and Lord Thackeray was placed in a carriage with the Duke and Duchess. He seemed to be through the worst of his fevers, but they still came and went. Bridget prayed he would make a full recovery.

The dock gangsmen were untying the ropes from the quay and preparing to sail again.

This was goodbye, she concluded. Some people were not good at saying the words. Perhaps it was for the best.

Bridget stood like a statue as she watched England recede into the distance. The wind caught the sails and they moved quickly out into the Channel. When she could no longer see the coast, she decided to go down below, into one of the cabins, to cry in private. It was very kind of the Duke to arrange for her passage back to Ireland. She could not have afforded to take her family home if not for his kindness—certainly not in this luxury. It was dark down below deck, but she did not care. She felt her way into the cabin and to the bunk that had been hers. That was when she sensed she was not alone. Had her maid decided to take a nap? Perhaps she did not feel well due to the choppiness of the waters. Bridget felt around and lit a candle, only to see Tobin sleeping on the bunk. He must have passed out from exhaustion and missed getting off the boat in Portsmouth!

"Tobin," she said as she shook his arm to wake him up. "Tobin! You forgot to get off the boat!"

A pair of green eyes opened and looked up at her. "I did not forget, lass. You did not think I would really let you go alone, did you?"

CHAPTER 9

*N*ow, if you don't mind, lass, I need my beauty sleep. We
have a few hours before we reach Ireland. I suggest you
sleep, too." He closed his eyes.

"Tobin!" she shouted.

He sighed dramatically. "I knew that would not be the end of it."

"You cannot be here with me. This is not proper!"

"Hang propriety! Think of me as a servant and then no one will
care." He closed his eyes again, but he could feel her staring at him. He
could not simply turn over because of where his wounds were. "There
are other bunks, lass. I was not asking you to share with me."

"I did not mean here and now, Tobin. I mean when we reach
Ireland."

"We can worry about that when it happens. We have but a few
more hours of peace before we must see about burying your father
and brother."

She closed her eyes but nodded and then climbed on to another
bunk across the small cabin. There was little more than wooden walls
and beds built into the walls. It was not far enough away. Tobin could
still smell her scent and feel her pain, and when she began to cry, he

was undone. She tried to muffle her sobs, but he would have known it anyway. Something in the air changed.

He crawled out of his bunk, ignoring the searing pain in his head and the strong wave of nausea that overcame him when he moved. It did not help that everything was spinning about. They could not be off the boat too soon for his comfort.

"Lass," he whispered as he knelt down beside her bunk. He swept the hair off her forehead and taking out a handkerchief, wiped at her tears. It seemed their roles were reversed for once.

"Forgive me," he whispered. "I did not mean to be harsh."

She shook her head. "There is nothing to forgive." She inhaled a few ragged breaths as she tried to stop her tears. "That is the truth of it."

"It does not mean I have to be a crabby ogre."

"True," she said, but did not argue.

He chuckled softly. "That's my lass. What has happened is more horrible than anyone could have imagined."

"I have never considered I might, one day, be truly alone. You know it can happen, of course, but what are the odds of them both dying in the same battle?"

"I know. It is unfathomable."

"Now I am all alone, I do not know what to do." She rolled over, away from him. "Go and rest, Tobin."

"I cannot do that now," he muttered, getting up awkwardly and sitting on the side of her bunk. He rested his elbow on his knees and, holding his head with one hand, stroked her back softly with the other. It was grossly improper, but his mam had done much the same when he was a child and he knew it soothed. He would do whatever it took to comfort Bridget during her grief. He did not know what would happen after that.

"What is waiting for you there, lass?"

"I do not know," she whispered. "I have not been there in almost ten years."

"There is a house?"

She nodded.

"And the elderly aunt lives there?"

"As far as I know, she still lives."

That was inconvenient, Tobin thought to himself, but he would not stay long. Hopefully, they could make shift despite the presence of the old woman.

"Tobin, you cannot return with me unless you marry me first."

"You know I cannot do that."

"Then you must return to England with the ship," she commanded.

"Once I have seen you safe and settled, I will return."

"You do not understand. If I return unmarried yet in your company, my aunt will force me."

"You are of age. She cannot force you to do anything."

"Unless something has changed drastically, she can and she will. It is her house and her money. Unless my father left me more than my dowry, I will have no choice."

Tobin did not know what to say. At times like these, he hated the aristocracy. "Did she have someone in mind?"

She barked a laugh, so different from most ladies of her station. "It does not matter. Perhaps I will be fortunate in my father's will. Go back to your bunk and sleep, Tobin."

He would sleep now, but that was the only instruction he would obey. He had letters from the Duke of Wellington and Waverley to help with the solicitors. He would wear his uniform and be acting in their stead and if the crotchety old aunt did not approve, then he would take Bridget away from there.

Despite his musings Tobin slept, because his body forced him to. His last thought, as he drifted away, was the hope that the nightmares would stay away this time, but he feared returning to Ireland would cause new ones. Even if he saw people he knew, no one would expect him to be an officer, and people saw what they expected to most of the time.

He awoke when they docked. He had slept hard. It was dark in the cabin and he did not know if Bridget was still there. He did not want to light a candle and wake her if she was. He crept out of the cabin and climbed to the deck to find she was already up and watching them berth. They had travelled all night and dawn already past. It was grey and cloudy, threatening rain… very much how he remembered his homeland.

"Good morning," he said as he joined her against the railing.

"Good morning. I expect this is goodbye. Thank you for accompanying me here and for being my friend throughout everything," she said stoically.

"I am not leaving you, lass. You might as well accept it. Besides wanting to see you safely established, I have letters from Wellington and Waverley to deliver to your father's solicitor."

"You are like a leech that will not loosen its grip."

"I have been called worse, but that is apt. I knew you would discover soon enough you did not want me."

"You know that is not what I meant." She shook her head and turned away.

As soon as they had pulled into the quay, Tobin left the ship and went to arrange for transport. He hoped they would not have to ride with the coffins. Dungarvan was not a large port, but they were not too far from the village. The people there were familiar with Lord Dungarvan's manor house and happy to help, especially when they heard what the errand was.

He had decided it would be best for him to take a room at the local inn and behave as though his interest in Bridget was purely professional, as a representative of Wellington and the army. Surely, her aunt could not object to that?

By the time it was all arranged to Tobin's satisfaction, the wagon was to arrive to transport the coffins as soon as the carriage pulled away. The less Bridget had to see, the better.

Dungarvan was a beautiful place. The O'Neill family was from the north. Tobin had never liked that his mother had chosen to give him his father's surname, though it made little difference. He was still a bastard.

Bridget said nothing as they rode through the picturesque coastal village, the quay filled with fishing boats, and multicoloured houses lined the streets. They passed into the countryside which was as lush and green as he remembered.

"Not long now, if memory serves," Bridget remarked as she looked out of the window.

"Shall I go in first and pave the way?" Tobin asked.

"It would do little good."

Hours later, the carriage turned into a tree-lined drive which overlooked a beautiful valley. Tobin felt a sinking feeling that this was going to be no simple cottage or house. The grounds rivalled Waverley.

Tobin stepped from the carriage to hand Bridget and her maid down, then he directed the driver to wait for him. He would need to return to the village to seek an inn and the solicitor.

He turned to find Bridget waiting for him, standing in front of a large, grey stone mansion. She was still the most beautiful woman he had ever seen, but the fire had gone out of her. She had receded into herself somehow. There was no longer a sparkle in her eye or a smile. Dressed in her mourning blacks, he supposed it was only natural, but he had a sinking suspicion it was something to do with the aunt who lived in this house.

He held out his elbow for her. "Shall we go in?"

She took his arm but hesitated.

"It is not too late to leave, lass."

"I warned you not to come, Tobin."

"I have never been any good at obeying directions," he teased.

"My aunt is a bully," she said quietly.

"Then you will have to be strong, lass." He gave her hand a squeeze where it lay on his arm. "I will not leave you to the wolf."

She looked up at him, resigned, a sadness in her eyes, before she took a step forward and knocked on the door.

Tobin had a troubling sensation his acting skills were about to be put to a severe test.

~

So MANY MEMORIES intruded upon Bridget that she struggled to maintain her composure. Many happy memories with her mother had happened during visits here when she was a child. That, of course, had been long before the horrible time she had spent here one summer, when her aunt had tried to force her to wed… Bridget had written to her father to come and fetch her. She had been only sixteen and grieving the loss of all she had ever known when her father decided army life was no longer suitable for her. Looking back, she understood why her father had left her there. It was no easy life, following the drum—especially without a mother—but Bridget still believed anything was better than living with Aunt Betha.

An unfamiliar butler opened the door, looking displeased that anyone would call so early. It was early at half eight, but Bridget had little patience for society hours. This was not Town.

She handed the butler her card as she walked past him into the entrance hall. "I am Miss Murphy, her ladyship's niece, and this is Lieutenant O'Neill. We have brought my father's and brother's remains home from Waterloo for burial. If you would be so kind as to inform her we are here, we will wait in the drawing room."

The dour man bowed. "Yes, Miss Murphy."

Tobin followed her, holding his hat under his arm. He was looking a little better every day, and he had removed his bandage this morning, covering his wound with his hair.

The house had changed little. It still smelled of a mixture of mustiness and beeswax, masked with fresh flowers. The same pink velvet curtains hung from the tall ceilings above the windows, while a rug with matching pink, gold and blue hues showed wear. Uncomfortable wooden chairs were placed around tables in groups for entertaining. It felt stuffy, which suited its owner perfectly.

Bridget walked to the window where Tobin was standing and looked out at the view of a river forming one boundary and rolling hills another. It was beautiful outside.

Half an hour later, the butler announced her aunt. "Lady Dungarvan."

Bridget began to feel guilty as she turned to see a shrivelled old woman, stooped over a cane.

"Well, gal, I imagine you are regretting not marrying Riordan now."

The guilt faded quickly. Her aunt hobbled forward and found a seat.

"It is good to see you too, Aunt. I hope you are well?" She did not mask the bitterness in her voice.

"Do I look well? I cannot stand straight and every joint is rheumatic. Are you going to introduce me?"

Bridget closed her eyes for a second to find some courage.

"Lady Dungarvan, this is my friend, Lieutenant O'Neill. He risked his own life to recover Father and Patrick."

Tobin stepped forward and bowed. "My lady."

"Any relation to Wrexford? I can see that you are," Lady Dungarvan said, surveying him through a quizzing glass and not giving him a chance to answer. "You escorted her alone?"

Bridget answered, "My maid is with me. The Duke and Duchess of Waverley accompanied us as far as Portsmouth. They had undertaken to see Lord Thackeray safely home."

Her aunt grunted her disapproval.

Tobin stood near the window, his hands behind his back, observing. Why had he stayed?

"So, your father and brother managed to get themselves killed, and you have come back to beg my forgiveness. I have not changed my mind. If you do not marry Riordan, then you are not welcome here, or to your inheritance."

What did she have to say to Bridget's inheritance?

"I have merely come to bury Father and Patrick, ma'am."

"And then what will you do?" she snapped. "You have nothing to offer anyone else."

Bridget saw Tobin shuffle a bit.

"Be that as it may, I do not intend to trouble you with my presence beyond the funeral. I must attend to the arrangements at once. I will take a room at the inn and not inconvenience you further. Will it be acceptable to bury them beside Mother?"

"Still as insolent as ever! You will do no such thing. As if you can parade about town unchaperoned with Wrexford's boy and stay at an inn without tongues wagging. No one has ever had cause to call me inhospitable and they will not start now."

She looked at Tobin. "You, too, soldier. Have your bags brought in."

"It is no trouble to stay at the inn, ma'am. I have errands to run in the village."

"All the more reason to stay here, then. You did not bring your horse or carriage with you, did you? No; that is what I thought. I will hear no more about it."

Tobin glanced at Bridget. She had little sympathy for him. She had tried to warn him.

He bowed and clicked his heels. "I will be off to the village to visit the vicar. I assume he resides near the church I saw when we docked?"

"Yes, that is the one. He is deaf as a door nail."

"As long as he is available to perform the service with haste, I do not care much what else he is or is not," Tobin replied.

"I want to go with you," Bridget said, knowing her aunt would try to argue. "I wish to have a say in the service. Just because we must make haste does not mean it should be without taste."

"Just so," Tobin answered and held the door for her.

"We will return this afternoon, Aunt. Please do not trouble yourself over us or rearrange any of your plans. We will not be staying long."

Bridget hurried through the door before her aunt could find a reason to keep her there.

As soon as they were back in the carriage, Bridget exhaled a heavy sigh.

"She is a bully," Tobin remarked.

"You have only seen the surface of it," Bridget warned.

"Do you truly intend to leave here?" Tobin asked, looking concerned.

AN OFFICER, NOT A GENTLEMAN

"I can only hope, but much will depend on what the solicitor has to say."

"Where else can you go?" He was scowling now.

"That is not for you to worry about. I will contrive something."

They arrived at the vicarage, and the vicar was, in fact, quite deaf. He could still speak, but the conversation was mostly one-sided. He read lips a little, it seemed.

"Good morning," Bridget said as they were shown into a study by a housekeeper. The vicar was plump with a friendly face and stood to greet them with a smile.

"Welcome!" he shouted.

"Reverend, I am Miss Bridget Murphy, Lady Dungarvan's niece. I have come with sad tidings. I need you to perform the funeral for my father and brother as quickly as possible. They fell at the Battle of Waterloo and I have brought them home to be buried beside my mother."

"A funeral, you say?"

"Yes, two together. My father and brother," she said slowly. "As soon as possible."

The man looked confused, and Tobin walked over to the desk and pointed to the pen and paper lying there.

"May I?"

"Yes, please. Forgive me; I am a little hard of hearing." Tobin and Bridget exchanged amused glances.

Tobin explained in writing what they needed, and it was arranged for the next morning. Bridget was grateful Tobin had been there. He surprised her by handing the vicar some words to read out from the Duke of Wellington himself.

"Oh, this is jolly good of him! I only knew the general a little, myself. Good man, of course, but this makes it personal, Lieutenant. Well met."

"I am glad to be of service, sir," Tobin said loudly. They shook hands and took their leave, once again feeling relief to be leaving somewhere.

"Do you wish to return to the house or do you want to see if the solicitor is available? I can see him myself on your behalf," Tobin offered.

"I appreciate your willingness to help, but it is not necessary. You should go back and rest."

"To the lion's den alone? Nay, thank ye. I told you, I am not leaving you yet. Certainly not before the funeral. Now, where do we find the solicitor?"

Bridget pulled out of her reticule a piece of paper with the address written upon it. Tobin took it and read the direction to the driver before climbing into the carriage.

"I could have handled all of this for you, lass."

Bridget nodded. She did not want to tell him she would do anything to avoid being alone with her aunt. The Lion's Den was an apt description.

They arrived at the offices of O'Brien and Flynn, Esq. Bridget's hands were shaking as they were shown into the small but tidy office. She had never been anywhere like this and so much of her future depended on what he had to say.

"Good afternoon," a gentleman said as he stood up behind his desk. "How may I help you?"

"Good afternoon, sir. I am Miss Bridget Murphy and this is Lieutenant O'Neill. My father and brother fell at Waterloo. I have come to request the execution of my father's will.

"The funeral is to be held tomorrow morning," Tobin informed him. "Here are some letters to verify the claim Miss Murphy makes, although I do not think there is anything to contest."

Mr. Flynn frowned as he looked through the letters Tobin handed him. "My father handled the accounts for the Murphy family."

"May we see him, then?" Bridget asked.

"Unfortunately, my father perished in the same fire which destroyed all the records several years ago. We sent notices to all of our clients. However, your father would have been given a copy of the will at the time it was made. Unless you have that copy, I am afraid I cannot help you."

Bridget stared at the man.

"What is to be done if she cannot find the copy?" Tobin asked.

"I was expecting the funds from my dowry to be released to me to live on," Bridget explained.

Mr. Flynn looked acutely uncomfortable. "Whenever there is no will to direct the distribution of funds, it goes to the Chancery Court to make sure there are no other claims to any of the property left by the deceased. I am terribly sorry."

Bridget nodded and walked out as if dazed. She could not trust herself to speak. It felt as though a nail had been driven into her own coffin.

CHAPTER 10

*T*obin helped Bridget into the carriage, then climbed in after her. Instead of taking the opposite seat, he sat next to her and pulled her into his arms. He was so very tempted to offer her marriage, but they would be no better situated. In the eyes of Society his name would not be considered respectable, and she was not accustomed to living in the manner prescribed by a lieutenant's pay. Tobin had no other income. Perhaps he should consider the business offer Major Fielding had made to the brethren last winter, in Paris.

She rested her head on his chest and it was the sweetest sensation he could remember.

"Have you looked through your father's belongings? Could a copy of the will be there?"

"I have no idea. My aunt might have it—not that she would give it to me."

"I suggest we return and look through his possessions. Is everything here with you?"

"No. We kept a small house in London. I suppose there is a chance he kept some papers there."

"I can write to Waverley and request a search to be conducted, if that is acceptable to you?" he asked. "I am sure he would know where to seek the appropriate authority to do so."

"That would be most helpful. I can include a note for the butler. He and his wife keep house there year round."

Tobin nodded, but his head was beginning to throb and he was experiencing strange, swirling lines in his vision. He tried to ignore it, but could not keep his hand from lifting to his temple. Slight pressure seemed to help a little.

"Your head is hurting. You will go to bed as soon as we return," she ordered.

"As soon as we return, Miss Murphy, I will first write the letter to Waverley and then help you look for the will."

She shook her head. "You are too stubborn for your own good. I would like to plead a headache myself to avoid dining with my aunt."

"Then you should. The sooner we find the will, the sooner you can leave."

"If only it were that simple."

Tobin feared he would have no choice but to go to bed with this megrim. He was having them so often he wondered if this was his future—that and the nightmares.

"Why did you not deny being Wrexford's son?" she asked.

"Because I am."

She looked up at him, perplexed.

"His natural son, lass."

She vaguely remembered Waverley mentioning something of the sort. "Oh…" She broke off, looking apologetic. "Is that why you left Ireland? Forgive my inquisitiveness. If you do not wish to talk about it, I quite understand."

"Yes, 'tis why I left. 'Tis complicated."

"Did he acknowledge you?"

Tobin hesitated. "In his own way. He paid for my keep and sent me to school, where the legitimate sons reminded me every day exactly what I was."

"Why must children be so cruel?"

"Do not be sad for me. 'Twas where I learned to fight and look out for myself. It came in most handy when my stepda would take his anger out on me."

Bridget gasped.

"Aye. He had no care for the bastard son."

"Did he treat your mother and sister that way?" She sounded angry.

"Occasionally Mam would get hurt if she came between him and me. And when I misbehaved, he never failed to remind her that he took her in with a bastard son. A priest's granddaughter, she was, reduced to shame."

"Are you still close to her?"

"I was, but it was easier for her if I stayed away. Now that she is a widow, she would not be punished for me calling."

"Will you visit her before you return to Wellington?"

"I do not know. I fear I will remind her too much of Wrexford. Your aunt was right. I look just like him, and she is happy now."

"What mother would not want to see her son? She must think of you and worry every day! Forgive me. Your head aches and I am badgering you about something which is none of my business."

"I will be thinking on it, *begorrah*."

They had already arrived back at Dungarvan House and Tobin felt the same sense of dread Bridget did. He did not wish to mingle with a cantankerous old hag, but he also did not want to abandon Bridget.

Hiding his reluctance for her sake, he stepped down from the carriage. The sunlight instantly caused sharp pains behind his eyes. He shut them again as far as was possible while still being able to see, but the pain was almost unbearable.

"You must go to bed at once. I insist." Bridget's brow was furrowed with concern.

"Maybe just for a while," he conceded.

The door opened for them, and as they climbed the stairs, he could see she was hoping that her aunt could somehow be avoided. There was no sign of the aunt, but another familiar and unwelcome face loomed above on the landing.

"Greetings, Cousin. Mama tells me you have come to your senses and have agreed to a wedding." Tobin would have instantly hated the man if he did not do so already. He was tall and handsome, with a smug smile on his face—the same smile he had worn two decades ago when he had ganged up on him with Wrexford's heir. Bridget instantly tensed and clutched Tobin's arm.

"I have done no such thing, Cousin. Lord Dungarvan, may I present, Lieutenant O'Neill? He was the brave soul who brought Father's and Patrick's bodies to me."

"O'Neill," the smug blackguard said as he inclined his head. "My thanks on behalf of the Murphy family."

"Now, if you will forgive us, Riordan, Lieutenant O'Neill is still suffering from a head wound. I intend see him safely to his bedchamber and then join you for dinner later."

Bridget turned away, still grasping his arm.

"Hurry back. We have much to discuss, Cousin," the man called after her.

She turned her head and coolly considered him. "The only thing on my mind is burying my father and brother tomorrow. Do I make myself clear?"

"Perhaps you should make yourself clear to Mama. She sent letters to the entire family, informing them we would be married quietly, after the funeral, in order to respect your mourning."

Even Tobin tensed at that. He would steal her away before he would allow Bridget to be forced into something against her will. Bully was too nice a word for the termagant... and Tobin could not think of an appropriate word to describe her son. If the offer had come from almost anyone but Riordan Murphy, Tobin might have tried to encourage Bridget to marry. Then he could leave knowing she would be well provided for in the bosom of her family. He knew, however, that to leave Bridget with her aunt and cousin would be to consign her to a dire fate. Equally, to watch her marry Murphy would be akin to ripping his heart from his chest. The only other person who Tobin deemed would be as heinous a husband was Wrexford's heir, Kilmorgan. Tobin's head hurt too badly for him to think deeply upon a solution, but he knew he must help her soon.

Bridget said nothing more but began walking down a long hall to some bedchambers. Entering one, she found his belongings had already been placed inside.

"This is your chamber. Mine is just across the hall if you need me. Now sit and I will help you get comfortable." She gently pushed him until he fell on the bed.

"Lass, you cannot be in here. I can valet myself," he protested, though his tone did not offer much protest. He had little energy to argue.

She sat down on the side of the bed and began to pull his boots off. "Let them find me in here!" she said through gritted teeth.

"I am sorry. I wish there was more I could do to help you." He brushed a lock of hair off her forehead.

Bridget stared at him for a long time before answering. "You are here with me. That is enough." She tucked him into the bed fully clothed and then went over to draw the curtains so the room was shuttered in darkness. Crossing to the wash-hand stand, she poured some water from the porcelain jug into the matching basin and returned with a damp cloth for his forehead. "I will return presently with a draught for the pain."

"I will think of something, lass." Tobin fell into a deep sleep almost at once and scarcely noticed when Bridget returned to give him the draught.

BRIDGET WAS SO angry she had to pace up and down the hall for some time before she was calm enough to confront her aunt. This was exactly why she had run away all those years ago. She even had a strong suspicion that Aunt Betha had her father's will and knew she held her niece in her control. On that thought, Bridget went to seek out her father's belongings. The trunks had probably been loaded on the wagon with the coffins. Bridget enquired of the butler and was directed to the stables.

She grew more frustrated as she walked. How dared the woman? How dared her aunt take away Bridget's ability to properly bury her family and even mourn them? There was no good reason for her aunt to insist on this marriage—except at one time she had decided it would be a good idea and no one ever thwarted Aunt Betha's will. Even Cousin Riordan, who was now Dungarvan, bowed to her every command. The former lord, her father's elder brother, had been a sweet old dear, but had been happy to keep the peace.

It was some distance from the house to the stables, and she passed the chapel and graveyard where two graves were being dug. Swallowing hard, she tried to divert her mind to the new stone building ahead with beautiful, arched wooden doors and large beams overhead. Everyone in Ireland bred horses, and the new, elaborate edifice was a testament to where the priorities of this family lay. A groom greeted her and directed her to one of the stalls inside the stable.

It was an odd place for such things to be stored, considering how large the house was, but Bridget immediately began rummaging through the trunks of clothes and personal paraphernalia—a task she was not prepared for. Every item of clothing or property brought back a memory of her father. On the top were his dress regimentals, which he had worn the night of the Duchess of Richmond's ball when Bridget had refused to go... That had been the last night she had seen him. The last time she had danced with him had been at the Waverley ball, the night she had also met Tobin. The thought of Tobin brought a small smile to her face. Now he was the man she wanted to marry, only how could she convince him?

She shook her head and continued to search for her father's papers. It was surprising how little her father truly had in the way of worldly goods, though very little was needed to be a soldier. Bridget thought he had the right of it, for only consider her aunt—she had every worldly possession but no happiness. She was a dried up, bitter old woman.

Bridget closed the trunk with sadness and looked for her brother's.

He had been her best friend—no, her sole friend in the world. She opened his trunk, not expecting to find anything, but needing to be close to him. His dress regimentals were also there and she brought them to her face to inhale his scent. She sobbed at the unfairness of a life lost too young. He was so handsome and charming... it was always said God took the good ones much too soon.

Knowing she had been gone too long, she rummaged through the rest of Patrick's trunk while she tried to dry her tears. At the very bottom was a packet of papers and Bridget opened them in haste, her fingers shaking with hope.

Inside was his certificate of birth, his commissioning paperwork, and finally, his will and testament but not her father's. She scanned the document for the line she needed, which was thankfully short.

Upon my demise, all of my worldly possessions I leave to my sister, Miss Bridget Murphy.

Bridget held it to her chest. Would it be enough? She tucked the papers back into the satchel and stood, brushing the straw from her skirts. Bridget needed to have a candid discussion with her aunt, and considered what she should say on her way back to the house. Frankly, she had little expectation of a reasonable discussion, even though it had been ten years since the first time Aunt had tried to force her hand.

Bridget wanted to find her aunt alone, so she hurriedly changed for dinner and sought Lady Dungarvan out in her apartments. The Tartar's maid told Bridget that her aunt had already descended to the drawing room. Unfortunately, she was not alone there.

As Bridget entered, she held back a gasp. It seemed her aunt had gathered, at little notice no doubt, every remaining family member in the vicinity. She should not have been surprised, since Riordan had evidently answered the summons from who knew where.

"I was wondering if you were going to snub us," her aunt said caustically.

"No, I have been attending to business matters regarding Father's and Patrick's deaths. I am sorry if I have kept you waiting."

"And the Lieutenant?"

"He retired to bed earlier with a severe megrim caused by his head wound. I would be very surprised if we see him before morning." Bridget turned to look at her family members. "Good evening,"

"I am sorry we are meeting on such a sad occasion." Stepping forward to kiss her cheek, Uncle Fergus looked so much like her father that Bridget had to choke back a sob. She glanced around at the faces of aunts, uncles and cousins, wondering again how her aunt could expect her to marry the next morning. Maybe Riordan had been jesting. She looked to him and he raised his brows with an amused twinkle in his eye as he saluted her with his glass before taking a sip of sherry.

There had to be a way to stop this nightmare.

Uncle Fergus took her arm. "I would like to hear about Waterloo, if you feel up to telling me. All I know is what the papers say."

"Lieutenant O'Neill is the one you should ask, Uncle. He was there, running dispatches for Wellington, and was injured in the same blast that took Patrick." She wiped a tear away which escaped down her cheek. "He brought him back to me in Brussels so I could be with him at the end."

"Oh, dear girl. What you must have been through! And to bring the bodies back alone... You are to be commended." He turned away to compose himself.

"I was not alone. I had a great deal of help from Lieutenant O'Neill, Captain Elliott and the Duke of Waverley. They escorted us as far as Portsmouth, but had another injured soldier to return to England." She bit her lower lip. "Father died during the final charge, I am told, along with almost his entire regiment."

"And now you are all alone." He took her hand and squeezed it with affection.

"She is not all alone." Her aunt scowled. "The whole family is here in support, are we not?"

"Yes, thank you, Aunt. It seems I might have to intrude upon your hospitality longer than I anticipated. There was a fire at the solicitor's office and all the records were lost. Until I find my father's will, I shall be unable to leave; unless you think it might be here?"

"What do you need with his will, niece? You will marry Riordan."

The dragon was showing her claws already, was she? Well, Bridget had some too. She shook her head decisively.

"No, Aunt Betha. I will not be marrying my cousin. I declined the offer ten years ago, and nothing has changed."

Her aunt's face was red with anger. "You have no choice, you insolent girl!"

"If wanting to marry the man of my choice makes me insolent, then so be it, ma'am. It also begs the question, why do you wish for the match so strongly?" She turned to her cousin. "And you, Rory?" she asked, using his childhood nickname. "Why are you submitting to this tyranny?"

"I want only what is best for the family," he answered smoothly.

"I too, wish the best for this family, but I must also do what is best for myself."

"You will have not a penny if you do not marry Riordan!" her aunt threatened.

Bridget furrowed her brow as she considered this statement. "I fear you are ill-informed, Aunt. Father told me, just before he left for the battle, that he had left me well provided for and I still have my dowry. If we cannot find the will here, I have someone who will send it from London." Bridget was bluffing, of course, but her aunt did not need to know that. "It might take a few extra days, that is all. However, I am in mourning and intend to honour my father and brother properly."

"Well met, niece," her uncle whispered in her ear. "Do not let her force you into anything."

She smiled sadly at him. "It makes no sense to me," she admitted.

"It makes perfect sense if you know the truth, though I know ladies do not know of such things." He hesitated and then whispered, "Riordan prefers men and always has. That is why she thought to force you so young and why again, even now. Do not give in, my dear. I will help however I can."

"Thank you, Uncle." Bridget was too stunned to say else.

"I will not stand for this!" Her aunt thud her cane on the floor. "You will marry Riordan after the funeral and that will be that."

"I am afraid that will not be possible..." Everyone turned towards the new voice. Lieutenant O'Neill stood on the threshold, looking marvellously handsome in his regimentals. "...for she already belongs to me."

CHAPTER 11

$\mathcal{T}$he silence was near deafening as all heads turned towards Tobin.

"What? Why did you not say aught of this earlier?" the old witch demanded.

"There was hardly an appropriate time, Aunt Betha. All my thoughts have been centred on Papa and Patrick, and helping Lieutenant O'Neill recover, not on my wedding. I need not add Papa and Patrick both approved of him, of course."

"Then we will wish you happy, Bridget," said an older man who looked much like her father.

"Thank you, Uncle Fergus," she replied with a warm smile.

Tobin had not intended to intrude on the family gathering—for it was that without a doubt. There were a dozen people in the room and he wanted nothing to do with them. He had awakened from his megrim-induced sleep and having found Bridget's note to her servants in London, had wanted to post the letter to the Duke with all haste. It was when he was returning from that errand he had overheard the old lady trying to force Bridget's hand. He knew he had to come to her rescue and now understood why she had pleaded with him to marry before they arrived.

"No! This cannot be. It must not! There has to be a way to undo it." The old lady snarled like a wild boar.

"I am afraid not, Aunt Betha. We are both of age and have consented."

"Why do we not eat our dinner and allow Bridget to mourn in a proper fashion? I find your remarks grossly distasteful," Uncle Fergus said sharply. Tobin wanted to applaud. At least there was one person willing to stand up against the woman, who was clearly used to manipulating this family like marionettes.

Tobin was allowed to escort Bridget into dinner. She said nothing but cast him a grateful glance. They would determine the rest later. For now, he had to help her survive this ordeal.

Whether or not it was intended, Tobin sat at the corner with Fergus on one side and Bridget on the other. A shy cousin named Eileen sat across from him.

Mostly, Fergus monopolized the conversation, wishing to hear the details of Waterloo. Those at that end of the table sat and listened while Tobin described the horror without dwelling on the reality of that dreadful day. Bridget sat quietly next to him and said little except for after Tobin had finished.

"Two days later, I rode to the battlefield. It was still very apparent what had happened there despite the sunshine and quiet. I found the scabbard to Father's sword where he fell," she said quietly.

Tobin then reached under the table and took her hand. She squeezed it hard.

They decided to retire early with the funeral being arranged for the next morning. Tobin walked Bridget to her bedroom. Pushing open the door, he stepped inside and pulled her into his arms. Comfort and support was what she needed now. She began to speak, but he silenced her. "We will resolve everything later, lass. I could not let the old witch ruin your life."

She pulled back and smiled at him. "I was only going to say thank you for rescuing me." She stepped up on tiptoe and gave him a soft kiss.

"I am no hero, lass. I should go to my own room now," he said, giving her a devilish grin that he had not felt like using in some time. "Good night, *mo álainn.*"

The next morning was sombre, as funerals had a habit of being. It was a small, quiet service at the family chapel, with a few people from the village also attending. The coffins had been kept in the ice-house, but there was no question of opening them.

The vicar shouted out the service, and Tobin stood up to read the letter from Wellington. It was short and simple.

The coffins were taken outside to the freshly dug graves and lowered into the earth. Tobin held Bridget's hand, knowing that although she appeared strong, this was the hardest part.

The vicar bellowed the familiar words as he cast some dirt upon the coffins:

"Forasmuch as it hath pleased Almighty God of his great mercy to take unto himself the soul of our dear brothers here departed: we therefore commit their bodies to the ground; earth to earth, ashes to ashes, dust to dust; in sure and certain hope of the Resurrection to eternal life, through our Lord Jesus Christ; who shall change our vile body, that it may be like unto his glorious body, according to the mighty working, whereby he is able to subdue all things to himself."

Tobin stayed by her side as the last few words were spoken and the rest of the people returned to the house, and then held her while she cried.

There was a small spread of victuals awaiting them at the house when they returned. A few people from the community that had known General Murphy attended and paid their condolences to the family. Tobin mostly kept to the corner, though there were those who came to pay their respects and express their appreciation for his service. Two things were on his mind as he stood back and observed. The first thought was where was the old hag hiding the will, and the second was how quickly could they leave this place. Tobin had known why Lady Dungarvan wanted to marry her son to Bridget as soon as he saw the lordling again. Riordan, along with Wrexford's heir, had often tried to force Tobin to join in their... activities. Tobin wondered if they still enjoyed each other's company. Then he dismissed the thought. He did not care what Wrexford's heir did. He wanted nothing to do with either of them. Lost in thought, he stared out of the back window until someone interrupted his musing.

"I never thought to see you again, son."

Tobin only just avoided jumping at the words. He turned slowly to look into the aged face of the man who had fathered him. It had been so long since Tobin had seen him, he had not noticed him among the assembled.

"Wrexford. I *hoped* never to see you again," he said with as little emotion as he could muster. To be fair, Wrexford had never done anything to him, but had done little for him other than to send money.

"You still hate me," his sire said plainly.

"Why are you here, sir?" Tobin asked, equally frank.

"Lady Dungarvan informed me you were here, but I knew of your successes from Wellington. We knew each other at school. He was quite complimentary of you. He said you were one of his finest officers. Imagine my surprise when I heard that, after you refused to let me purchase you a commission."

"I have never asked anything of you," Tobin said, unable to mask all the acid in his voice.

"No, but I would have given you anything I could. I loved your mother, you know."

Tobin was so angry, he wanted to plant his fist into Wrexford's face, but settled for clenching them.

"I should have tried to put things right much earlier, but when I lost Kilmorgan, my eyes were opened to a great many things. My father took you away from me, in essence, but now I have the opportunity to remedy some of it."

"I did not know he had died," Tobin said softly. Much though he hated his brother, he could see the torment in his father's eyes and his heart softened a little, although he did not know what Wrexford meant about his father. "My condolences."

"Thank you. If you and your wife have time to visit before you return to Wellington, I would be grateful for a few days with you. There are some things I would like to tell you."

Tobin could feel his scowl. Just because Wrexford's heir had died and he said a few kind words did not erase the past nor mean Tobin wanted a future with the man who begot him.

"I would like to do my best to set things right with you."

"I will think about it," Tobin said as Bridget came up to him and slid her arm through his.

"Will you introduce me, son?"

Tobin wished he would stop calling him that.

"My Lord Wrexford, this is my wife, Bridget O'Neill."

His father took her free hand and bowed over it. "My son has done well for himself. Welcome to the family, Bridget."

She inclined her head coolly. "Thank you, my lord."

"I have been trying to make peace with my son and convince him to come for a visit. Perhaps you can persuade him it would be in his best interests. Life is short, as you know, and my estate is not above twenty miles from here." He bowed, then abruptly took his leave.

"What was that about?" Bridget asked as they watched him go.

"I do not know," Tobin confessed. "Your aunt told him I was here. Kilmorgan is dead."

His head was beginning to hurt again and he did not want to think about what had just happened. He had hated his father and brother for so long it had become second nature. Wrexford had said the right words, but was he in earnest? Tobin was not certain he was ready to forgive.

AT THE WAKE, Uncle Fergus stayed by Bridget's side whenever Aunt Betha came near. For some reason he had decided to protect her, but she was grateful. After everyone had paid their respects to her, he pulled her aside to a nook in the drawing room.

"Do you really think there is a copy of your father's will at the London house?" he asked.

"I wish I knew for certain. There were no papers of any kind in his trunks. There have to be some somewhere. He would not lodge everything with his man of business, surely? Why do you ask?"

"I have a suspicion Betha is plotting something, and I strongly suspect it has to do with Riordan marrying."

"Surely there will be someone willing to marry him for his title alone?" Bridget countered.

"No doubt, but no outsider would be invested in keeping it a secret as family would be. If that knowledge were made public, he could be hanged. I wonder what she will try now that she knows you are ineligible?"

"I certainly do not wish for him to be hanged," Bridget said. She and Rory had been playmates, once upon a time. Perhaps that was why her aunt thought she would be tolerant of his tendencies. "Hopefully she will let me go in peace. Do you think she has legitimate claims on my father's will?"

"I would not think so, but she might be hiding it in order to constrain you."

The solicitor said that without the will we will have to go to the Chancery Court. It could take months."

"At least you have your husband's military pay for now," he said reasonably.

"That is true," she said, feeling quite guilty for dragging Tobin into such a mess. She looked over to where he was conspicuously hiding in the corner and smiled. An older gentleman went up to speak to him and Tobin tensed.

"Who is that man speaking with my husband?" Bridget was astonished how quickly the lie flew off her tongue. Perhaps it was because she wanted it to be true.

"That is Lord Wrexford."

Bridget took a closer look. The man looked exactly as she imagined Tobin would in twenty years' time. Tall, handsome, distinguished... "I should have guessed."

"The resemblance is remarkable. It is a pity about Kilmorgan."

Bridget was confused. It must have shown.

"His heir died last year. No one really says why, other than illness. He and Riordan were close."

"Tobin looks uncomfortable. Perhaps I should rescue him." She was about to walk away when her uncle took hold of her elbow.

"I will try to have a discreet search for you."

She met his gaze with a look of what she hoped was appreciation. "Thank you, Uncle. I fear I will need all the help I can get."

She walked slowly across the room, trying to determine if she would be intruding. All she knew was that Tobin felt animosity towards his father, yet it appeared as though Lord Wrexford felt no shame in acknowledging him. So far, it did not seem that her family was aware Tobin was illegitimate. Now, would that titbit not put her aunt in a pucker!

Bridget quietly placed her arm through Tobin's and Lord Wrexford asked for an introduction. This deception kept getting deeper and deeper. Bridget had no qualms about deceiving her aunt—it was tit for tat—but the more people who knew, the harder it would be to undo and keep her reputation intact.

The next thing she knew, Lord Wrexford was inviting them to visit. Bridget was unsure how she felt about the man. If he had really mistreated Tobin's mother, then she wanted nothing to do with him. His mother had been a priest's granddaughter and he had made her his mistress—it was badly done of him. However, he claimed to want to make peace and he had a genuine, repentant look in his eye.

She sensed his temper was ready to ignite. "Shall we walk outside?"

He gave a slight nod and patted her hand on his arm. The gardens were in full bloom on this warm, summer day. A hint of rain was in the air, making the fragrances at their best.

"How are you faring?" Bridget asked warily, unsure of how Tobin would react.

"I cannot think of what to make of him," Tobin answered.

"Would it hurt to hear him out?"

"I do not know. I have spent so much time resenting him it has become a pastime."

"How much did you see him when you were younger?"

He sighed. "I have not set eyes on him since I was five, and not often then. Yet there is no denying it: 'twas like looking at my own reflection."

"A few years in the future, but yes," Bridget agreed. "Everything you know about him is from your mother, then?"

"No, not all. Wrexford's heir and I were sent to the same school together. Our father's idea of a joke, I am sure."

"Perhaps he had hoped you might be friends."

"Quite the opposite, I assure you. If I had not been a year older and bigger, I hate to think what would have become of me. What do you think he wants?"

"I can only speculate," she answered. "Maybe he wishes to know you better and it is as simple as that."

"My mam said very little about him, but when she did it was always in private. I would not want to leave here until things were resolved with your father's will," he said, putting his fingers to his temple. Bridget wondered if he noticed he did that when his head was paining him. She could tell it was from the particular crease between his brows and the way he half closed his eyes.

"Uncle Fergus said he would try to look for the will discreetly, of course. He thinks my aunt has nefarious reasons for wanting me to marry Riordan."

"Well, he cannot have you," Tobin snarled.

"Oh, Tobin, what if they find out?" She looked up into his eyes.

"Hush, lass. I will protect you." He gazed back at her with such tenderness, she wanted to understand.

"Why will you not marry me in truth?"

"Because you deserve someone who can give you the moon and stars, not a tent and a pallet."

"I am content to be a soldier's wife, Tobin. You know that."

"What about when we have bairns? We might be fortunate enough to have peace now, but there is no guarantee."

The thought of having children with this man made her stomach flip. This was right. They were meant to be together.

"We have discussed this."

"Yes, and I find all your arguments foolish. I was brought up following the drum. What would you say if I obtained my dowry and the London house? Would you be too proud to live off my funds? It happens all the time in Society," she argued.

"I will not abandon you, but there is a proper gentleman out there for you. I know it."

She looked heavenward and closed her eyes. "I do not want a proper gentleman. I want you." She wanted to strangle the stubborn man. He may not realize the truth of the matter, but she was ruined for any other man. Perhaps she could find someone in Ireland to take her who lacked knowledge of aristocratic society, but there would be a scandal if she attempted to become a part of the *ton*. That position held little interest for her, but Tobin was dear to the Duke and Duchess of Waverley. In all likelihood, with his looks, charm and connections he could look higher than her for a wife but did he know it? As she mused, they walked on past the gardens, down to the river.

"Do you think your aunt keeps her documents in a locked chest or drawer in the study? I was considering having a nose about tonight after everyone is abed."

"I do not know, but my Uncle Fergus means to hunt for Papa's papers. He would have more of an excuse than you if caught."

"Do you trust him?"

She sighed heavily. "As much as I trust anyone here, I suppose, other than you. He seems to have my best interests at heart. He even warned me that my cousin does not care for women and he believes that is why my aunt is so insistent Riordan will wed me."

"He told ye? Were ye much shocked? Nay, I don't suppose you were, though 'tis not something a gentleman would generally sully a lady's ears with." He paused, looking thoughtful. "Has the old Tartar said any more since I told her we were married?"

"Not in my hearing. I have avoided her whenever possible."

"I do not blame you. I am tempted to visit Wrexford's estate for a few days, just for some relief, while we await news from Waverley. I would like to see what your uncle finds first, though."

"Do you mean it? We would probably need to tell Wrexford the truth. I do not wish to carry the lie beyond here. Your father moves in Society, as do you."

"Only when I know you are safe from the *cailleach*."

Bridget laughed at him calling her aunt a witch. "And for that, I will be forever grateful to you—as if I were not already forever in your debt."

Tobin turned her to face him and tilted her chin up so they were looking eye to eye. "I wish you would not think that way. Think of everything you have done for me. May we call ourselves even and lucky to be such good friends?"

"Friends," she whispered with a sinking heart.

CHAPTER 12

*T*obin had decided he did not trust anyone in this strange family. He thought it the best thing that could have happened to Bridget, being brought up away from them. While he waited for the house to grow quiet, he thought for a long time about what she had said. Would it be possible for them to be happy together, given the disparities in their stations? He wished it could be true.

Remaining in his stocking feet for stealth, he crept out of his room, along the corridor and down the grand staircase to the study. Sneaking about, spying in dark corners, reminded him of his time in France. He had preferred it to shooting people on the battlefield. Yet what would he do if he sold out of the army?

It was a question he needed to answer soon, but first, Bridget had to be taken care of. He had promised.

As Tobin drew closer to the study, it was obvious someone else was there. He could hear drawers were opening and closing and papers being shuffled. If someone was attempting to look for something, they were not being very secretive about it. Tobin tried the handle and finding the door unlocked, opened it to see that the unskilled spy was Bridget's Uncle Fergus. Tobin entered and stood in front of the door for at least five minutes before the man looked up.

"Lieutenant O'Neill," Fergus said, not in the least bit alarmed that he had been caught at his task. "I am searching for Dónal's will for Bridget."

"Any luck?" Tobin asked.

"A little, perhaps. I found my eldest brother's will and it certainly explains why Lady Dungarvan wishes Riordan to marry Bridget. If he marries before his thirtieth birthday, he receives his inheritance at once. If he marries Bridget, he also receives title to all the unentailed properties."

"And if he does not marry her?" Tobin asked, knowing the answer.

"The unentailed property goes to me as the last surviving male. It would have gone to Dónal if he had not fallen at Waterloo."

Tobin nodded. "Then it seems we will have to wait for news from London. Have you searched everywhere in here?"

"I believe so," the man said, looking around at the mess he had made. "There is a safe in the master's bedroom, but that will be trickier to access."

It would not surprise him one bit if that was where the document was, Tobin thought. Short of drugging Riordan, and his valet, it would not be an easy task to access it.

At least, Tobin realized, this uncle had reason to keep Bridget from marrying Riordan, so he trusted him to be self-serving enough to help Bridget for the nonce. He returned to his room to seek a few hours' sleep, and spent much of that time going back and forth in his mind over whether or not to visit Wrexford.

He finally fell into a fitful sleep—and the nightmares intruded again.

Tobin was riding Trojan across the battlefield at Waterloo. Smoke from the Château Hougoumont fire hung thick in the air, choking him and making his eyes sting. The stench from all of the dead and wounded lying in the mud and heat was growing noxious. Through his exhaustion, there was a hint of hope that the Prussians were coming and the battle could still be won that day. Dimly, through the black fog, he saw a hand lift and Tobin rode towards the familiar face. He had just reached Captain Murphy when the deafening sound of a cannon exploded and shook the earth next to them.

Tobin flew through the air, hitting the ground with a painful thud, then Murphy landed on top of him... except when Tobin came to, Wrexford's heir was looking down at him with a snarling, pox-riddled face and was taunting him, laughing dementedly while trying to pull him down into the fires of Hell.

Suddenly, he was a boy back at school, and Riordan was there, helping Liam hold him down. Tobin began to fight and claw at the devil on top of him.

"Tobin! Tobin, stop fighting me!" a familiar voice shouted. He was being held down and writhing hard as reality returned.

"Bridget?" he whispered, trying to catch his breath.

"Yes. You were having a nightmare, Tobin."

"Doona' leave me," he said through chattering teeth and fearful tremors. His body was soaked with sweat.

"I will never leave you, *mo grá*," she whispered in his ear. "It was only a bad dream. You are here with me in Ireland and you are safe." She continued to whisper to him until gradually her words broke through the fevered imaginings of his mind and he began to calm. Then, realizing she was lying on top of him as though trying to hold him down, he became very aware of his carnal needs. He opened his eyes to see her dark midnight gaze watching him in the dim light of a taper.

"Lass, did I hurt you?"

She shook her head. "Do you wish to tell me about it?"

He shook his head and she leaned down to kiss him.

He was only human and all the desires he had suppressed flooded his being. Finally he could acknowledge he was starving; desperate for her as though the devil was truly coming for him and these were his last moments on earth.

Their mouths clashed and devoured as though their last meal was each other. His hands began to roam over her back and she planted kisses all over his face and neck. His Bridget clung to him as though she understood, and her passion matched his, kiss for kiss. However, some little voice deep inside kept reminding him that the time was not yet right. She was not his.

"Lass. Lass. We must stop."

She ignored him. "Will you marry me if we do not stop?" she asked, gazing down at him with a devilish, most unladylike grin.

"No proper man would have done this to you."

"That argument grows old, Tobin."

"So ye were trying to seduce me?" He grinned at her in his turn.

"If I thought it would work, I might." She blushed. "I suppose I became a little carried away."

"You have no idea how much of a saint I am being at this moment. Let us hope Saint Peter remembers when I arrive at heaven's gate."

Lifting her away from him, he tucked her into his side. Of course, Bridget, being who she was, could not resist looking at his wounds when she was so close to them.

"You appear to be healing well on the outside. How do you feel on the inside?"

"At this minute, I feel as though I am about to explode."

"Oh. Oh..." At last she understood the effect she was having on him. "Perhaps, then, it is better if we stop for now."

"For always," Tobin said, regretting the words the moment they were spoken. Was he truly such a great fool as to let an angel go? Yes, he was, but he would do it because it was best for her. Despite her words, she was still clinging to him and he was not ready to let her go yet. He wanted to savour these moments and store them for later.

"I found your uncle in the study."

She lifted her head and looked at him. "Did he find anything?"

"Not your father's will, but he found the late Earl's. Apparently, if Riordan marries at all he receives his inheritance immediately but if he marries you, he retains control of the unentailed properties."

Bridget gasped. "I cannot believe my uncle would have put such a clause in his will!"

"Can you not?"

"No! He was a kind, dear man," she protested.

"But he did whatever the witch wanted."

"Sadly, that is true. What happens to the unentailed properties if he does not marry me?"

"They go to your Uncle Fergus."

She frowned. "It makes his motives to help me less pure, does it not?" She put her head back down on his chest.

"To be fair, they would have gone to your father."

"But Riordan is young. In all likelihood, he will outlive Uncle Fergus just like he did my father."

"Perhaps there is more to it than I know. I did not read it—I only know what your Uncle Fergus told me."

"I do not want to stay here, Tobin."

"You do not have to, lass. I was thinking we could visit Wrexford for a day or two while we wait for word from Waverley." Tobin was growing tired and Bridget was snuggled down on his chest.

"That sounds wonderful. Can we leave in the morning?" she asked in a sleepy voice.

"As soon as possible," he agreed, knowing she was not going to leave his room this night. He reached over and put out the taper between his thumb and forefinger, then pulled the tangled sheets back up over them. He only hoped he could maintain his saintly behaviour until morning.

BRIDGET WOKE up and realized she had fallen asleep in Tobin's arms. What had possessed her to do such a thing? Then she remembered his nightmare and blushed at her brazenness. She inhaled deeply, relishing his scent and his warmth, and looked forward to the day when she might wake up with him every morning. Reluctantly, she crawled carefully out of the bed and crept back to her own room to dress for the day, instructing her maid to have their belongings packed for an early departure.

When she left her room, she found Tobin standing waiting for her in the hall, arms crossed. She smiled and raised up on tip-toe to kiss him on the cheek. His devilish little half smile made an appearance and she could see in his eyes he cared for her, even if he wished to deny any deeper feelings. It was enough of a morsel to keep her hopes alive for now.

"I want you to distract Riordan for a while so I can search for the safe. Your Uncle Fergus said there was one in Riordan's room," he whispered in her ear. It sent shivers down her spine. Did he know what effect he had on her?

"He may not be awake for some time," she remarked.

"Then we will wait. I think it is worth the effort before we leave. Who knows what kind of plan they might hatch while we are away?"

"I was hoping we might not have to return at all," she murmured.

"Perhaps so, if we are lucky. I need to stop in the village to have them re-direct my mail to Wrexford unless I return."

She squeezed his hand and smiled at him. She hoped they would be able to obtain her dowry, at the very least, but she would have to convince him the money did not matter. Even to her own ears, she knew it sounded naïve, but she had lived before in less than ideal circumstances and had been happy.

When she entered the breakfast room, she was surprised to find her aunt and cousin in close conversation. What were they plotting? They both sat back hastily when they saw her and Riordan came around the table to greet her with a kiss on the hand.

"Good morning, Cousin," he said with his customary smooth smile.

"Good morning, Riordan; Aunt Betha."

"Might I make you up a plate?" he asked.

"No, thank you, I only want toast and tea at the moment."

"I have some correspondence to attend to," Aunt Betha said, and Riordan went over to help her up. Bridget did not miss the pointed look her aunt gave him. Something was afoot.

Riordan sat down, folded his hands across his lap and stared at her. It was awkward, to say the least.

"You need not wait for me, Cousin," she finally said.

"I was hoping you would take a turn about the garden with me when you have finished your repast."

"Tobin and I are leaving to visit his father at Wrexford for a few days, so I must not tarry."

"It will only take a few minutes. There are some things I must tell you."

She narrowed her gaze but thought of Tobin searching Riordan's rooms, and agreed. "A short stroll, then."

She rose, put her napkin on the table and went with him out into the garden. When they were some distance from the house, he cleared his throat and began.

"I overheard you and O'Neill talking yesterday. You were not very discreet."

"I do not know what you mean, Rory," she prevaricated.

"Very well, I will be direct. You are not truly married, are you?" His gaze bored into her.

"We were betrothed before the battle and said our vows on the ship. We intend to renew those vows when we return to England, but in every other sense of the word we are married."

"Not in any way that would be considered legal in court," he said, looking very pleased with himself.

Bridget felt the hairs rise on the back of her neck and a growing sense of panic. "You cannot force me, Rory," she pleaded with her childhood friend. "Uncle Fergus told me about the codicil to the will."

He paused, as if gathering his thoughts, and then shrugged carelessly. "You cannot blame me for trying. We were good friends once, and you would have all the freedom you could want. You could even keep your lieutenant if you like."

"How gracious of you!" she retorted sardonically.

"It would be a marriage on paper only. You would not even have to touch me, though I suppose, for a female, you would be the one I could bestir myself for an heir or two." He took his hand and softly ran his fingers down her cheek. She was going to vomit.

"I could pass his babes off as mine, although I could wish it were someone other than Wrexford's bastard. Come, Mama and the vicar are waiting in the chapel," he said, taking a hard hold of her arm to lead her away.

"Rory, I cannot," she said, at the same moment something flashed before her eyes and Rory collapsed to the ground.

"Keep your hands off her," Tobin growled. Looking astonished, Riordan clutched his nose, which was spurting blood.

Bridget handed Riordan a handkerchief and then grasped Tobin's hand. "He knows. He overheard us in the garden yesterday."

Tobin cursed. "Never mind. We need to leave before they force you," he said. "The trunks are packed and the carriage is waiting."

"I really must insist you stay, I am afraid," Riordan said. As they turned towards him, he cocked a pistol. "Please unhand my bride."

The sound of another gun being cocked came from behind them, and Bridget faced about to see Uncle Fergus pointing a fowling piece at Riordan.

"I do believe they have a carriage waiting," he said. "Go now, Bridget." He inclined his head towards the front drive.

"Bad cess to all of ye, you gobshite crazy ejeets!" Tobin said, pulling Bridget away and setting off almost at a run. Reaching the front drive, they climbed into the carriage, where Bridget's maid was sitting up on the box next to the driver. "Make haste away from this hell-hole!" Tobin shouted before he shut the door.

They were down the drive and out into the countryside before either one of them said anything. Bridget's pulse was still racing with horror.

"Are you harmed, lass?" Tobin asked. "Thank God I wasn't too late!"

She nodded her head and her chin began to tremble. He took her into his arms. "I canna' stand to see you unhappy. But what am I to do with ye? I think we had better marry after all." He kissed the top of her head. "'Tis the only way to keep you safe. But only if you are certain."

She looked up at him, unable to stop the tears pooling in her eyes. "*Beggorah mo álainn.*"

"I know you think it is a mistake, but we can be happy together, Tobin."

"I will do my best to make you so. We will work it out as we go. I could never have seen any of this coming in a hundred years."

"They surpassed even my expectations," she confessed.

"I will ask Wrexford for help. Goodness knows, I have asked for nothing from him before. If he does not have the connections to see us married here quickly, I don't know who will."

"I am glad you are giving him a chance, Tobin."

He sighed. "I am not sure if I am being a fool or no. He seemed genuine, and I have seen too much loss in the wars. I expect I have grown soft."

"Being willing to listen does not make you soft. It makes you wise."

"That is something I have never been accused of." He laughed.

"I think you are caring and compassionate, and really quite wonderful." She wrapped her arms around him.

"Lass, what is going to happen when your eyes are opened to the real me?"

"You do not fool me one bit. You are the most unselfish, honourable man I know. You were my friend when I had no one else, you brought my father's and brother's bodies to me at your own peril, you have stayed with me to protect me from my family, and now you are going to marry me."

Tobin shifted uncomfortably with the praise. "I did what anyone would have done in my position."

She made a noise of disbelief. "Hardly. I am grateful, though, dearest Tobin. I will make you happy."

"You already do, lass. You already do."

CHAPTER 13

*T*obin was distinctly uncomfortable as they pulled in through the gates of the Wrexford estate. He had not known he was a bastard, or that he had a different father, until he was about five years old, when they had seen him in the street. Even then, he had not truly known what it meant until he had been sent away to school and the legitimate children had thought it their right to harass and beat the bastard. Wrexford's heir had taken particular joy in it. Perhaps it had been embarrassing for him, though Tobin had never told anyone who he was. Somehow, people had still known.

His mother had explained things to him, and through a child's eyes, he had often wondered what it would be like to live with his real dad in a grand house.

When he had come home from school, his stepfather had made it clear he disliked him. Tobin had never thought anyone liked him besides his mother until he enlisted in the army and became Waverley's man.

The estate was grand, just as he had expected it would be. It was a shame that there was no longer an heir. Not that Tobin cared for the aristocratic sense of entitlement, but good peers employed a great many people.

It took them some time to reach the house. It was more hilly than Dungarvan had been, but equally lush and green. The carriage climbed in order to reach the house, which stood proudly atop some cliffs, overlooking the Irish Sea.

For a brief moment, Tobin wondered what it would be like to own all of this. He had been born first, but on the wrong side of the blanket. Tobin was not sure he could forgive his sire. His mother had been genteel, if not a lady, and had deserved an honourable marriage. With a shake of his head, he dismissed those thoughts. He was here to make peace with his father if he could, but was not sure it was possible.

Bridget reached over and took his hand.

"It is very grand," he said, for lack of a better way to describe it. He had grown accustomed to manor houses while working for Waverley, but there was something different about this one. The mansion was an orange-pink stone, with mullioned windows and gables that seemed to change with the light.

"It seems desolate," Bridget remarked.

"'Tis certainly solitary. It is quite some ways from the village."

Nevertheless, a groom came out to take charge of the horses and a butler opened the door to greet them. Lord Wrexford was not far behind.

"Welcome home, my son," the man said, smiling.

"You were expecting us?" Tobin asked, surprised. "I should have sent word, but we left rather suddenly."

"I was hoping, shall we say," Wrexford corrected.

Tobin helped Bridget alight from the carriage and a strong wind from the ocean nearly pulled her bonnet off.

"And here is your lovely bride. You are most welcome," Lord Wrexford said to her. "Come inside and the servants will show you to your chambers. Would you like to freshen yourself or have some tea? This is Mrs. Byrne, she has been housekeeper here since I was a lad."

"Welcome," she said with a curtsy. Then she looked up into Tobin's face. "As I live and breathe, you look just like your father!"

"Yes, he does, Mrs. Byrne," Lord Wrexford agreed with a grin. "He's a regular chip of the old block!"

"And you are in mourning, you poor dear," she said to Bridget. "You must be tired if you have come all the way from Dungarvan. Come with me."

The plump, older woman with a shock of red hair led them up a majestic, white marble staircase to a landing where large windows overlooked the water. Steep cliffs formed in a horseshoe around the property and the waves splashed against the rocks into a white foamy spray.

"What a magnificent view! It reminds me of the Peninsula," Bridget exclaimed.

"You will have the same view from your rooms," Mrs. Byrne explained. "Some days I stop and stare at the majesty of it all and think of how fortunate I am to have lived in such a place." She stopped at the end of the hallway. "Here we are," she said as she opened a large wooden door into a luxurious chamber. The only thing Tobin had seen as luxurious as this was Waverley's chambers.

The rooms were decked out in pale shades of blue and gold. There was a large sitting room, set in between the two bedchambers with their adjoining dressing rooms.

"I hope you will find this satisfactory. Anything you need, just ring. Tea will be in the drawing room at your convenience and hot water will be along shortly."

"Thank you, Mrs. Byrne."

She smiled and bobbed a curtsy before closing the door behind her.

"What do you think?" Bridget asked.

"I think I am overwhelmed. To think I might have grown up here had circumstances been different."

"I have certainly never lived anywhere so grand," she replied as she joined him in looking out of the windows and took his hand in hers. They stood there in peaceful silence until a servant knocked on the door with hot water.

"You enjoy your bath. I think I will go down and speak with Lord Wrexford. I feel the need to get this over with."

"Are you sure you wish to do this alone?" she asked, looking concerned.

He gave a slight nod. "I think it is for the best. Enjoy." He gave her a quick kiss on the cheek and left, hoping he could find his father. When he arrived downstairs, the butler informed him Lord Wrexford was in his study and escorted him there. Tobin was nervous in a way he had not been before.

"Well, son, I am glad you have come. Can I offer you a drink? I confess I am somewhat nervous."

Tobin laughed. "That is good to hear, for my palms are sweaty and my knees are knocking."

His father went to a cupboard, poured them both a measure of whisky and handed a glass to him. He raised it.

"To finding each other again."

Tobin did not know how to respond but he raised his glass to his father's and then took a drink for false courage.

"Please have a seat. There are many things I should tell you."

"May I go first?" Tobin asked.

His father looked surprised. "Of course."

"Bridget and I are not truly married. Her aunt was trying to force her to marry Dungarvan, so we said that to protect her. Her cousin overheard us and discovered our deception, and this morning, they tried to force her into the marriage. Apparently, there was some addition to the will that Dungarvan would not retain the unentitled properties unless he married her."

"That sounds complicated," his father said, scowling. "You managed to get away unscathed, I gather?"

"Barely. We were searching for her father's will. He told her he left her well provided for, but the solicitor did not have a copy. We suspect the old lady was hiding it, but I wrote to Waverley to ask him to investigate at Murphy's home in London."

"Gracious heavens. I was not expecting any of this. What will become of Miss Murphy, then? None of this will have done her reputation any good."

"I plan on marrying her in truth. I cannot convince her I am not a worthy gentleman."

"Because you are my natural son, or because you feel you cannot support her?" his father asked bluntly.

"Both, of course. She is a proper lady of the highest character. She deserves far more than I can give her." Tobin spoke into his glass as he swirled the amber liquid.

"I think you sell yourself short, son. She approves of you?"

"She seems to, but is it because she has no one else and feels all alone?" Tobin shrugged. It was such a strange conversation to be having with a man he hardly knew. "I was hoping you might help me arrange it, sir. The sooner we are married in truth, the safer she will be."

"Of course. I will see what I can do. There are other things of which you should know."

Why was Tobin afraid he was not going to like what he heard?

"It may change nothing, but you deserve to know the truth." His father took a drink and looked away outside, through the window. Tobin waited.

"I was married to your mother when you were conceived."

"Dia ár sábháil!" Tobin found he was gripping the edge of his seat. "Why have I never heard this?"

Wrexford sighed heavily and set down his glass. "Because my father had the marriage annulled. I do not blame you for being angry. I will try to explain. Your mother and I met when we were young and had nothing more to consider than being in love. She was raised by her uncle, who was the priest at Wrexford. I was home from Oxford. It was the perfect summer—one of my fondest memories. My parents were away most of the time and did not see what was happening. Clara and I married and you were conceived."

"Needless to say, my father was furious when he discovered what had happened. He petitioned for an annulment on the basis of us marrying under-age without his consent and in the Catholic Church. It was granted and he sent Clara away with a generous pension. Her uncle found someone willing to take her, but I did not learn of your existence until you were five. Clara forbade me to see you."

As ucht Dé!

"My father forced me to marry as soon as the annulment was granted, and William was born about a year later. His mother died a few weeks after he was born. I was not a good father to him. In truth, I resented him and now he is gone."

Tobin had no words.

"Are you able to forgive me, son? I should have fought harder to be in your life, but Clara said it made things more difficult for you both. Nonetheless, she did allow me to send you to school."

Tobin saw the anguish on his father's face and saw no point in holding on to a lifetime of hate whether what he said was true or not.

"Aye, I forgive you."

"Then, hopefully, you will not mind that I petitioned the Crown to reinstate my marriage to Clara so you can be named the rightful heir."

BRIDGET FINISHED her bath and dressed for dinner, but Tobin had not returned, so she went on down to the drawing room. He was not there either.

She heard the men talking farther down the hall and moved towards the voices to join them. As she approached the door to the study, she heard Lord Wrexford telling Tobin his parents' marriage had been legitimate and he was petitioning the Crown to have him claimed as his rightful heir.

Bridget was going to be sick. She clutched her stomach as the reality of what was happening sank in. The tables were turning in the opposite direction and quickly. She did not know what to do. If Tobin's circumstances were truly changed, then he would need a wife of his own station. The gap between them would be far wider, if he were to be an earl, than it had been before. If only she knew about her father's will! It would hurt to let Tobin go, because she cared deeply for him. She knew he cared for her as a friend—he had said so—but it would not be enough. In a daze, Bridget began walking back up the stairs to her room. This was a hard blow, indeed. Now she better understood Tobin's hesitancy to marry her before.

Tears threatened, but she was too upset to fully cry—something she had done very little of since Waterloo. Yet what could she do? Despair did not begin to describe her feelings at the moment. She had lost not only her father and brother, but apparently she would have to fight her crazed family for what was her rightful inheritance.

She heard Tobin returning, so she looked in the glass. A positive fright, with red eyes and blotchy cheeks, looked back at her. Quickly she ran to the basin and began to splash her face with water. Would Tobin tell her? If he did, she could be nothing but happy for him. After the life he had led, he deserved every bit of this good fortune. Was she strong enough to do what was right?

When Tobin entered, he looked as glum as she felt. Was he not happy with the news he had heard? He threw himself into a chair.

Bridget frowned. "Whatever is the matter, Tobin?"

"Everything. I do not know where to begin," he replied with his familiar scowl.

"You were speaking with your father. What did he say?" She hoped she sounded calm.

"That he is going to try to have me instated as his heir."

Bridget tried to look surprised and waited for him to explain.

"He was legally married to my mother, but the old Earl was able to have it annulled because they were under-age and my mam was Catholic."

"Gracious," Bridget said, trying to control her emotions. "How do you feel about it all?"

"I cannot say. It made sense when Wrexford explained it, but I still cannot fathom such a thing. Very likely nothing will change."

"You will certainly still be you," she said kindly, "though if you become the heir to an earldom you will need to look higher than me for a wife."

Tobin growled. "Now who is being ridiculous? I do not know that I rightly want all of this, though Wrexford did say he had already signed over one of his properties to me. He says it produces a nice income if managed well. Do you have a fancy for being a farmer's wife?"

"I fancy being your wife no matter what you are, Tobin." That much was true.

He reached forward and took her hands. "I do not deserve you, lass."

"How did your father react when you told him we were not married?"

"He did not bat an eye, and said he would see to the arrangements."

Bridget nodded. A few minutes ago, that would have been a relief to hear. "I wish we would hear back from Waverley. Then we would know how to proceed."

"We will hear soon. At least we do not have to await our fate at Dungarvan. Speaking of which, my father would like to host a small gathering. Would you mind?"

"I have no objections as long as Lord and Lady Dungarvan are not on the guest list." She gave a wry laugh.

"I still think it is strange that she invited Wrexford to your father's funeral."

"I can only think she thought to strengthen ties with him by inviting him to see his son. Whatever the case, I am grateful she brought you and he back together. You might never have known the truth."

"Yes, I suppose so." He shook his head in obvious dismay.

"You had best dress for dinner," she said, rising from the sofa. "Everything will turn out, Tobin. Even if you are not made the heir, you have lost nothing."

"Like hen's teeth."

"What was that?" She looked at him oddly.

"I said I have gained me a wife and a house."

"Of course you did."

When they came downstairs to the drawing room, Bridget expected a quiet evening getting to know Lord Wrexford, but there was a messenger at the door.

Wrexford took the letter from the butler.

"It is for you." He handed Tobin the letter.

"It is from Waverley," Tobin said as he opened the seal.

Bridget struggled to keep from snatching the letter from his hands. She felt her heart speed up and her palms grow damp with nervousness. So much was riding on the will.

"Please say it is good news," Bridget said while Tobin was still reading. She could not bear it any longer.

Tobin shook his head, but finished reading before he looked up. "I am afraid not, lass."

"What is wrong?" Bridget asked quietly.

"It is about your inheritance," Tobin said. "Waverley said there was no will to be found in the London house, but took the liberty of consulting his man of business. He will petition for your father's possessions to be turned over to you as next of kin. However, your dowry is gone. That account was emptied some time ago."

Bridget could not prevent soft whimper of despair from escaping. "By whom?"

"He says the only name on the register was Murphy, so if your cousin stole it, it is virtually impossible to prosecute. I am sorry."

"Then it is fortunate my son and you are to wed. He will be able to care for you properly with or without a dowry," Wrexford chimed in.

Bridget did not feel fortunate at this unexpected turn of events, and was surprised at Wrexford's willingness to consider their marriage.

A second note was attached to the first for Lord Wrexford, and Tobin handed it to him before coming over to take Bridget's hand.

"I am sorry, lass. I know you were counting on that dowry, but we will find a way."

Bridget forced a smile and then noticed Lord Wrexford appeared to want to tell them something.

"Is it bad news, sir?"

"I do not know, but Waverley says they have requested Tobin's certificate of birth and that we should come to London before the appeal goes before Parliament."

"Why would it matter?" Bridget asked.

"So I can be paraded like a goose before Christmas to see if I am an adequate specimen," Tobin snarled.

"Something like that, I am afraid. Parliament can amend the letters patent or the courtesy title could be made a peerage in truth with a writ of summons. Otherwise, the title goes into abeyance upon my death."

"All dependent upon the marriage to my mother being reinstated," Tobin clarified.

"Yes. It would be hard to deny you as rightful heir with a valid marriage," he said. "But first, we will hold our small gathering to celebrate your home-coming."

CHAPTER 14

*S*omething was not right with Bridget. Ever since the day before, she had been morose. It was understandable following the news that her dowry was long gone, but she had been different even before dinner. Was she not happy about the possibility he would inherit? Tobin could understand that. He was not sure how he felt about it himself.

When he went down to breakfast, he only found his father there, dressed for riding.

"Good morning, son," his father said pleasantly as he looked up from his papers.

Tobin was not sure he would ever get used to hearing 'son'. He used to long for his real father, so why was he so reluctant to embrace him now?

"Good morning," Tobin replied, finding himself wanting to slip back into his Irish brogue though his father's speech held no more than a slight lilt. They had tried to break them of that habit at school; Tobin remembered well the lashings he had had when he refused.

"I would like to take you out to ride around the property and visit a few of the tenants," Wrexford said, as Tobin filled his own plate. Tobin had not been on a horse since the day after Waterloo. His wounds were healing, but they still pained him. He suspected a piece of shrapnel was, even at the moment, trying to rear its head from his thigh.

"I can try, sir, I have not ridden since receiving my injuries."

"Oh," he said. "I had not realized, although I do suppose the wound on your head is recent. Were there any others?"

"Four in total. I had some shrapnel lodged in my flesh from the blast," Tobin explained. "The one on my head was the worst."

"We can try and always turn back if needs be." Wrexford was perfectly understanding. He was nothing at all as Tobin had imagined him to be. The memories from seeing him as a child were vague at best, and Tobin realized he had formed his impressions of him from his experiences with Kilmorgan.

"I imagine you think it is premature to teach you about the estate, but I visited London and pleaded my case soon after your brother died."

Tobin felt his brows rise in surprise as he halted his forkful of kipper halfway to his open mouth.

"Wellington had already told me about you and your success, and I knew then that you would be capable to take over. Very likely you are more capable than Kilmorgan, who was raised to it."

Tobin was silent for a moment and sipped at some coffee without tasting it before he spoke again.

"What does my mother think of this? If you have me declared legitimate, would that not reinstate your marriage?"

"I confess I have been too much of a coward to speak with her in person after she did not respond to my letter. In fact, I had hoped to have an answer from the Crown and seek you out to let you know after the deed was done. Is that dreadful of me? I know it is very selfish."

"I think you should let Mam know," Tobin answered quietly. He was not sure how he would have reacted with a *fait acompli* from his father had he found him on the Continent, but now he was soon to have a lady wife, and Tobin needed to be able to support her in the life she deserved. Like it or not, he would do it for her.

"I have kept track of Clara, of course. I know she was widowed some years ago and has a daughter."

"My sister, Rachel." Tobin nodded. She was married with two of her own children so far, so at least the stain of becoming illegitimate would not harm her greatly.

"I had thought to present Clara with a settlement for what she endured. I know my father paid her off and sent her money to support you, but I have no illusions that it was adequate to support her, even now."

Tobin thought back to the small cottage he had been brought up in, compared to this grandiose mansion, and had no idea how his mam was supporting herself since her husband had died. He needed to find out. He had sent her money as often as he could since he had left home—Waverley had always been a gracious employer. Nevertheless, Tobin had not seen her in years and had it been enough to sustain her? Bridget was correct—he needed to remedy the fact that he had not seen his mam. He would like to take Bridget to meet his mother. Finishing his breakfast, he was a little excited about the thought and wanted to tell Bridget, but when he returned upstairs, she was not in her room and her maid thought she had gone for a walk.

Tobin frowned. There was no harm in that, of course, but why had she not even said good morning or left a note?

He decided to leave her a note so she would not think she had been abandoned. Bridget was used to being independent and she was also grieving. Tobin would not mind a little time alone himself, to think about all the changes that seemed to be happening without his control. It made him wonder how much control people really had over their own lives. They liked to think they did, but perhaps they were simply instruments of something greater and had little say at all. He could certainly believe that after witnessing Waterloo.

Tobin wrote a note for Bridget and changed into his riding gear. Rarely of late had he worn civilian clothing, and he realized how shabby his wardrobe had become. If it embarrassed Wrexford... well, it had been a reality for Tobin before.

Two large Irish grey hunters, some of Ireland's finest were being held by grooms on the front drive. Tobin hoped he did not disgrace himself. He was able to mount without too much pain and followed his father on the tour of the estate.

From one end of the property to another, Tobin did not wonder at the notion that a good deal of Dublin or London could fit within the boundaries Wrexford owned. There were miles and miles of rolling hills before they reached the home farm and tenant farms. The hills were dotted with sheep on one side and cattle on another.

Even there being only a possibility that Tobin could inherit was more than he could fathom. He knew nothing about running an estate or a farm. How many people would be dependent on him? No one had ever really been dependent on him other than his fellow soldiers.

They rode through the village, which looked much like any other, but it was named for his father's title. Thatched cottages with colourful walls were set one next to the other, the brilliant flowers of summer pouring out of their windows and crawling up the walls. Meanwhile, vegetable gardens filled the small spaces of land they had. A beautiful stone church with a steeple stood watch over the village, and small shops lined the High Street.

Wrexford waved to everybody and people waved back, not seemingly out of duty but out of genuine friendliness. Wrexford introduced Tobin to a few gentlefolk who stopped to talk to them, but he could scarcely take it all in. The village and its tenants seemed to be happy and well cared for. Tobin saw no signs of neglect, which again surprised him. Was his mother as well taken care of? The village he had been brought up in was not so far distant, but was not on Wrexford land as far as Tobin knew.

They passed by the vicarage on their way back to the house, and they were invited in for tea. Tobin did not know if he was ready to face that yet. Social niceties were, for the most part, beyond him. Thankfully, Wrexford declined but mentioned the gathering he was holding in his son's honour.

Tobin looked at his father in surprise, who did not notice his son's chagrin. They rode back a different way from that they had come, taking them along the dramatic cliffs which could be seen from the house. Even at the height of summer, the wind was a fierce force and Tobin could not imagine how the elements would feel in winter. He was beginning to tire and long for a rest on his lavish bed. He scoffed to himself at how quickly he was becoming used to luxury. Then, as they rounded a sharp curve along the path, Tobin spotted Bridget, sitting on a rock looking out over the sea.

"Would you mind if I stop here?" Tobin asked. "I can see myself back."

Wrexford looked over to where Bridget was, and gave Tobin a smile and a nod.

"Thank you for the tour," Tobin said, not knowing what else to say.

"This place is my pride and joy. I hope it will not be lost," Wrexford said sadly before urging his horse forward. Tobin slid off his hunter and walked painfully towards Bridget. He might have to trouble her to take some shrapnel out soon.

BRIDGET REGISTERED the sound of hoof beats in the distance, but did not look up. She did not feel like speaking to anyone. It was desolate out here on the steep, rocky cliffs and it matched her mood perfectly. She was angry with herself for being angry at her father and brother for dying and leaving her in this position. She knew it was irrational, but felt it nonetheless.

When Tobin appeared next to her on a horse, she was not exactly startled, but neither was she prepared for the leap her heart did at the sight of him.

"What is wrong, lass?" Tobin asked with a look of concern on his face. "Is this all too much for you?"

Bridget did not know how long she had been out there. When she had dressed this morning, she had not felt equal to facing Tobin or Wrexford. The hole she felt in her life was so large she did not think it would ever be filled. She wanted to go back to Brussels, where things had been more simple. It was incredible she could think of army life in those terms, but it was what she knew. Now it felt as if she was losing the only person who really knew her and who gave her hope.

"I do not know how to answer that. I have been thinking." She watched a wave come in and crash against the rocks below, sending spray some hundred feet into the air.

"This is a good place to think, I would imagine," he replied.

"Tobin, I think we should delay getting married."

"The divil ye say. Am I hearing ye right?" His green gaze bored into her. She had fallen deeply in love with him. Did he suspect?

"You are not mistaken. Everything has changed." She picked a piece of clover near her hand and began to tear the heart-shaped leaves apart.

"Including your feelings for me?"

"That is not a fair question." She had not expected him to ask it.

"Is it not? That is how I felt when you asked me to marry you the first time. Here, I thought I would have someone to go through this with me."

"A friend," she whispered.

"Yes. No one else will understand me the way you do."

"I do not know if that is enough."

He was scowling. Bridget could feel it without looking up at him. "What about your crazed aunt and cousin?"

"I have no intention of going anywhere near them. I will wait for the courts to give me what is left of Papa's estate."

Now he was pulling up the clover and looking out over the sea. He was scowling and angry, but still looked more handsome than any other man she had known. She was aching with love for him and could not, in good conscience, marry him before the court ruling.

"Have you made up your mind, then?"

"I think it is for the best. You did not really want to marry me, anyway."

"Do not be ridiculous, lass. Who would not want to marry you? At least now I can provide you with a proper home."

Bridget wanted to scream, but held her frustration inside.

"My father has planned some grand party to introduce me to the neighbourhood." Tobin shook his head. "You had better not abandon me. I know you love these things as much as I do."

Bridget remembered the first time she had seen Tobin, at the Waverley ball, and smiled with sadness. How much easier things had been then. Had it only been a few weeks? Bridget's heart sank even further, if that were possible. She knew Tobin would not want a fancy Society life, and neither did she. A simple cottage in the country would do very nicely. Secretly, she prayed that the Crown would deny Wrexford's request to make Tobin heir.

"Can we wait to decide, Bridget? You will not leave me to face this alone, will you?"

She smiled at him. The least she could do was wait. He had done so much for her. She took his hand.

"Of course not."

"I confess," he said, his devilish smile returning, "I was rather beginning to look forward to being married."

Bridget was too, if she were being honest. Tobin held out his hand and helped her to her feet.

Leading the horse behind them, they walked back holding hands, their fingers entwined. He seemed to be as lost in his thoughts as she was. Bridget was even less certain of what to do now.

When they arrived back at the house, there was a carriage and four pulling up in front of the majestic façade. Bridget wondered if she could escape up to her room. She was not in a state of mind to be sociable.

"Should we turn back to the cliffs and pretend we did not see the visitors?" Tobin asked, a sly grin on his face.

Bridget laughed. "Did you read my mind?"

"I wish I could admit to such kindness, but the idea was purely selfish on my part. Do you think it will be a visitor only for Wrexford?"

"I sincerely doubt it, since he paraded you through the village. Word spreads faster than fire in the countryside," Bridget answered.

"Very well." Tobin seemed to groan the words through gritted teeth.

"Is one of your injuries plaguing you?" Bridget asked as she took the more proper position of placing her hand on Tobin's arm. Although everyone thought them betrothed, she did not want to cause more reason for talk now that they were within view of the house.

"There is no point in pretending with you," Tobin said on a sigh.

"None at all," Bridget agreed.

"It is my cursed thigh. Riding for hours this morning did not help," he admitted.

"Very likely it is a piece of shrapnel surfacing. I should take a look at it." She pulled off her glove and placed the back of her hand on his forehead and then his cheek. "You are a bit warm. Fevers often accompany irritated wounds. You will most likely experience this for some years."

Tobin nodded. He knew that from stories of other soldiers. "But first, we must brace ourselves to do the pretty. Who do you think it will be?" he asked. "A nosy vicar's wife? Are they not often the town gossip?"

Bridget laughed. Her brother had been the only other one to amuse her so. "Indeed, or the great lady of the county, since your father has no wife."

"Shall we wager on it?" His eyes were dancing with merriment.

"Ladies do not wager." She clicked her tongue with mock scorn. When they were alone like this and enjoying the absurd, she wondered if they would do all right together no matter poor or wealthy, titled or not. Was it wrong of her not to want to share him?

"A penny for your thoughts," he said as they reached the terrace steps.

She was afraid to voice her thoughts, but they poured out anyway. "I am afraid things will change too much," she confessed.

"They already have, *mo álainn*. Please do not lose heart on me. I cannot face this without you." He bent down and was kissing her lightly on the cheek when the door opened.

"There you are at last!" Wrexford exclaimed. "Come in and meet my sister, Lady Butler. She lives on a nearby estate."

Tobin and Bridget exchanged glances and he gave her a slight

138

wink. Entering through the terrace doors, Bridget saw a very fine lady, garbed in an ensemble clearly from one of London's finest modistes. Unfortunately, she was not alone. There were two young women with her. One was a beautiful, dainty blonde with ringlets for miles. She blushed when Tobin was introduced to her. The other girl was equally pretty with bright red hair and large blue eyes. Bridget suddenly felt very shabby in her mourning blacks. She had dyed her last practical gowns, not wanting to spend the little money she had on a new wardrobe.

They exchanged curtsies when Bridget was introduced and she did not miss the militant gleam in their eyes when Lord Wrexford said Bridget was Tobin's betrothed.

"It is hard to believe you are Wrexford's eldest son. I do not believe Father ever mentioned you or your first wife before," Lady Butler said.

"Father was a tyrant," Wrexford said, "but what is done is done, and I do not wish to speak ill of the dead. I only hope things can be rectified now."

"We will be leaving for London soon," the lady announced. "We were there in the spring and Ruby had many admirers."

"I have no doubt," Wrexford said, not rising to his sister's bait. "I intend to take my son and his wife to London after the wedding, if they are amenable. They should be presented at court and to Society by me."

The ladies smiled falsely. Bridget wondered if anyone else sensed it. Men often missed women's subtleties.

Begrudgingly, Bridget had to admit she liked Wrexford, but she knew enough about women to know she could do without his sister or her daughters. Perhaps she should suggest they visit Dungarvan. She happened to know someone who was desperate for a wife, she thought ungraciously.

CHAPTER 15

$\mathcal{A}$fter a tedious dinner with his new aunt and cousins, Tobin felt wretched. His body was burning and aching like the devil and he was so warm he could not get comfortable. Night-time was becoming something he dreaded though, because the terrors of war crept in. He escorted Bridget to her room but decided to wait until morning to ask her to look at his leg. She had other ideas.

"Goodnight, *mo álainn*," he said as he kissed her cheek at her door.

"Not yet. You need to have your leg ready for dancing."

He felt a scowl pinch his face. "I was hoping to use it as an excuse."

"Perhaps you will, but not before I see if there is something I can do. Go and make yourself presentable and I will fetch my medical bag."

Tobin was exhausted, but she was right. The longer they delayed, the more it would fester.

Tobin took off his coat, waistcoat and boots and then did his best to expose his wounds discreetly for Bridget to examine them. He still marvelled at her medical abilities.

She knocked on the adjoining door in their suite of rooms and, entering at his bidding, placed a bag next to him on the bed.

"I have brought you some of your father's best whiskey with his complements," she said with a mischievous grin.

"I think I was fortunate to have been unconscious the last time you went digging into my body."

"Undoubtedly," she agreed, "but as I do not tend to render you insensible this time, you had best fortify yourself."

"Yes, ma'am," he said, and took a healthy drink. It was not enough. Just watching her remove her instruments and dip them in the hot water that a servant had provided was enough to make him queasy. He drew on the bottle of Irish nectar. The Scots always claimed their whisky was the best, but Tobin preferred the smoother taste of the Irish to the mossy dirt flavour the men in skirts wore. To each his own, he thought.

"Take a deep breath," Bridget's voice commanded and Tobin obeyed.

"*As ucht Dé,* woman!"

"I know, and I am sorry, but a large piece of a cannon ball is trying to surface. I do not know how I could have missed this before." She frowned and two lines formed between her brows. Tobin reached up to smooth them out, but he found himself pawing at her face instead.

She laughed. It was a sweet sound.

"Are you ready? I need to prod again," she warned.

Tobin held up a finger, well he thought it was a finger but he was seeing more than one. He took another healthy drink and then nodded.

Curses again. Who was ever ready for that?

"I almost have it," she said and kept going.

Tobin continued to let out strings of muttered Gaelic.

"It is a good thing my ears are not delicate, Tobin. You would put the most hardened sailor to the blush," she chided.

"Most ladies would have swooned into a heap on the floor," he slurred. "And most ladies would not be performing surgery either," he said, rather shrewdly in his own estimation.

"An excellent point. If your new cousins are the standard for the ladylike ideal, I will pass on the nomenclature."

"They were quite ghastly," he agreed.

"Now I must cleanse your wound. I will take the whiskey, if you please."

Tobin held the bottle to his chest. "No. You will not waste this on my leg. Find something else."

Bridget glared at him, her hands on her hips.

"You look like me mam when you do that," he remarked. "Speaking of whom, I am to go and see her tomorrow."

Bridget walked across the room, pulled on the bell-rope and asked the servant to find her some less fine spirits.

She sat on the side of the bed while they waited. "Does your mother live close to here?"

"Less than a day's ride, I should think."

"So you will be back in time for your father's celebration?"

"We. We will go to visit me mam. About the celebration... I asked Wrexford to postpone it since you do not want to marry me any more." He rather thought he might be pouting, but he was beginning to feel very sleepy. Even so, he noticed she did not say anything.

The servant entered with another bottle and Bridget proceeded to burn him as surely as if she had held a hot iron to his leg. Perhaps that was what she was doing. Later, he vaguely remembered her wrapping his leg and tucking him in like a small child, with a kiss to his forehead.

The next day they set out for County Kilkenny. Tobin was nervous. They were silent for some time as they rode through the village in Wrexford's luxurious travelling barouche. Tobin was still dumbfounded by the thought that he might own this or his own carriage one day. What would his mam think when they arrived at her cottage?

"How is your leg this morning?" Bridget asked, interrupting his rapidly maudlin-turning thoughts.

"Much better, thank you. Did I say aught to bring you to the blush last night?"

"Nothing unforgivable, or that I have not heard before, I assure you."

"I am not sure if that is a relief or not," he muttered.

She smiled as she watched out of the window. Tobin could not say why he had insisted she come, but it had been her suggestion and for some reason it was important that she know where he came from if she truly wanted to marry. Although, he reflected morosely, even that was no longer a certainty.

"What is your mother like?" Bridget asked.

Tobin had to think. It was not easy to describe one's parents. "She is kind but tough; gentle but firm, hard-working and fair."

"She sounds like an ideal person, though I might describe you just the same."

Tobin cast a sceptical look her way. "And I you... though beautiful and compassionate come to mind when I think of you or look at you."

Her cheeks flushed. "Do you intend to tell her what is happening?"

"I have not decided. I suppose I want to see how she is."

"That is fair, but her life will change enormously."

"Aye, and I do not think she will like it."

"And how will she feel about becoming Lady Wrexford?"

Tobin stared at Bridget. "I do not know."

"If the marriage is reinstated, would she not be married again to your father?"

He gave a curt nod. "Perhaps, but let us not put the cart before the horse. Maybe it is not necessary to upset her unnecessarily."

Bridget remained quiet, giving him some much needed time to think, even though her presence comforted him. Everything was happening so fast. Did she sense it too? Was that her hesitation? She had become distant, but was it him, their situation, or her grief? It was often hard for soldiers to return to civilian life, and she might be no different. Yet what could he do about it? When she had mentioned postponing the wedding, a sense of panic and loss had hit him inside. If she did not wish for all of this, then neither did he. Quickly he was realizing it was more important to have her than anything else.

Tobin must have fallen asleep with his wondering, for when he awoke, the carriage was slowing to a halt.

He looked out of the window to see the familiar but strange cottage where he had been brought up. It seemed so much smaller now. The white stone was covered with ivy and the thatched roof was the same, but the trees were thicker and taller and the rose gardens were almost unruly with their riotous summer blooms. A deep pain inside made him want to turn and flee like a coward, but Bridget was there beside him.

"It is beautiful. I have dreamed of owning a house such as this one day."

"So meagre?" he asked doubtfully.

"It looks like heaven compared to most of our billeting over the years."

Tobin could not argue with that.

"Do you want to go in alone?"

"No," he replied immediately. He was using her as a shield, but she had become his rock; his comfort.

She reached around him and released the door. "Go on, then."

Tobin winced as he stepped down. Hours and hours in a carriage, no matter how luxurious, did not help a wounded leg be less stiff. He managed to straighten his face before he helped Bridget down.

She was looking up and smiling over his shoulder. Tobin swallowed hard and turned.

"Tobin?"

"Mam?" he questioned, but before she could respond she was in his arms.

BRIDGET FELT VERY MUCH as if she were intruding as she watched mother and son embrace. How could Tobin have doubted his mother's love? Although, she admitted, it was easy for Bridget to say that when she had never been the bastard child, or had a stepfather having been forced to raise her. No, she could not accurately put herself in Tobin's shoes.

"And who is this lovely young lady?" Tobin's mother asked, drawing Bridget's attention back to the present. Tobin's mother was younger than Bridget had expected. She had fair, strawberry-gold hair and bright blue eyes. She was still very handsome, but Tobin certainly looked like his father.

"Mam, this is Miss Bridget Murphy, my betrothed. Bridget, my mam, Mrs. Clara Brennan."

Bridget was surprised to hear him announce her so to his mother. She was also surprised when the lady took her hands and pulled her into an embrace.

"You poor dear. You have lost someone recently?"

"My father and brother at Waterloo," Bridget answered softly.

Mrs. Brennan pulled her arm through Bridget's and slipped the other into Tobin's. "Let us go inside. We have much to catch up on. I cannot tell you the relief I feel to see your face, Tobin. I have been reading the papers every day for the past ten years with the greatest anxiety."

They were soon seated in a small parlour that was neat, if a little shabby. A woman of all work entered with tea and some biscuits on a wooden tray. Bridget had no doubt she had noticed their grand carriage arrive.

"How have you been, Mam?" Tobin asked. His mother was still holding onto his hand, Bridget noticed, as if she did not believe he was real. Bridget took the liberty of pouring the tea and handing it to everyone.

"Tadhg died, but you have heard. I received your letters and your money, which has kept me comfortable. Rachel has two bairns now, but I know she has written to you."

Tobin muttered under his breath as he nodded.

"What made you decide to become an officer? I know your father offered to purchase you a commission and you refused."

Tobin was uncomfortable speaking about himself, Bridget could see. "Circumstances made it necessary... and it did not come from Wrexford."

"I read that his heir died last year," Mrs. Brennan said.

"We have just come from there. We are... ah... becoming

acquainted. I did not seek him out. He was at General and Captain Murphy's funeral at Dungarvan. He invited us to visit."

Bridget watched both of their faces as subtly as she could. Mrs. Brennan looked frozen, as if turned to stone.

Tobin let out a big sigh. "Wrexford is trying to have me declared legitimate so I can take his place one day."

Mrs. Brennan gasped and held her free hand to her mouth. "Is that even possible?" She looked bewildered.

"I do not know. I am not sure I even wish for it," he said candidly.

Mrs. Brennan stood and began to pace across the small room. "Would that mean my marriage was reinstated?"

Tobin glanced at Bridget with worry. "Would that be a horrible thing?" he asked.

"Oh, Tobin. It was so long ago. He has sent me letters through the years, mostly asking after you and providing funds for you, once he knew of you. I received one last month but I have not had the courage to open it for fear it was bad news of you."

The poor woman! Bridget knew she could not have stayed behind and sent her husband off to war.

"Perhaps you can open it without fear, now," Tobin said with his familiar grin. "As you can see, I am whole."

Mrs. Brennan walked back over to him and touched his face lovingly. "Injured, but still in one piece." She ran her finger down the scar on the side of Tobin's head as though it were a delicate flower.

"You have Miss Murphy to thank for that. She was brought up following the drum and has nursed many soldiers over the years. She has acquired some handy doctoring skills too, I might add."

Mrs. Brennan's attention settled back on Bridget. "Your losses were recent. Are you quite alone now? Tobin mentioned the funeral at Dungarvan. You are a relation?"

"I am Lady Dungarvan's niece. My father was the late Lord Dungarvan's second brother."

"You met in the army?" she asked.

"Tobin worked with my brother on the Duke of Wellington's staff. Patrick introduced us at a ball."

"You appear to be well suited, indeed." His mother beamed at both of them. "You have no idea how I have prayed for his safety and happiness. I am delighted he has found a good woman."

Bridget's heart was hurting to be deceiving this woman.

"I hope you intend to make an honest woman of her soon, son. You cannot gallivant around with a gently bred lady without sullying her reputation."

Tobin gave her a pointed look. How the tables had turned!

"It is I who chose to wait, ma'am. I wished to see the outcome of the ruling over his legitimacy. He might wish to pick a bride more suited to his station if he becomes Kilmorgan of Wrexford."

"Balderdash! If I know my son, his heart would not be so inconstant."

"Thank you," Tobin said with a wry grin at Bridget. "Do you not wish to open the letter from Wrexford?"

Mrs. Brennan looked at a piece of folded parchment lying on the small writing desk in the corner.

"I suppose it could not hurt, now." She picked it up and slid her finger under the seal before unfolding the pages and reading them. Tears were streaming down her face, accompanied by an occasional whimper, before she handed the letter to Tobin to read out loud.

My dearest Clara,

You may be wondering why I would write to you at a time like this, when it seems there is so much time lost. Our son is a grown man, after all. Firstly, as last I heard, he is well and alive and serving on Wellington's personal staff as a lieutenant. He has done well for himself, Clara.

Secondly, my condolences on the loss of your second husband. I hope he was able to make you happy. Thirdly, and to my point, I also lost my one and only son by my second wife. He was my heir. This brings me back to a painful episode in both of our lives, when our young love was torn asunder by my father. Tobin was born after the marriage was annulled, if my estima-tions are correct, and before I married again. I would ask that you send his certificate of birth so my efforts at instating him as my heir will be smoother. I have applied to Parliament, but the case will not be heard until the next session. Of course, there is the not insignificant matter that our marriage might well be re-instated as a result. Would this be an unpardonable insult to you, dear Clara? I would make you as comfortable as you wish, wherever you may wish, and you need not have any contact with me should you not desire it.

I await your assistance in righting a great wrong for our son.

Ever yours, etc.

Wrexford

Bridget moved to sit next to Mrs. Brennan, who had slumped onto the sofa and was trembling. Bridget put an arm around her and held her close while they listened. It was quite shocking news even though Bridget had heard it before. What would it feel like to think your marriage of a quarter of a century ago was still valid? It did not bear thinking of. She had lived another life with another man since then because Wrexford's family had abandoned her with a baby on the way —and now she might be a countess?

Tobin finished the letter and knelt down before his mother. She shook her head and wiped her tears away. Tobin held his handkerchief up to her face.

"You do not have to do anything you do not wish," he whispered to her.

"It is just such a shock. Of course, I wish for you to take your rightful place. Of course, I do."

She stood up, and walked back to her desk. Taking a Bible from a drawer, she opened the cover and pulled out two slightly yellowed pieces of paper. She handed them to Tobin. "Your certificates of birth and baptism."

Tobin nodded as he took the papers and placed them inside his coat pocket.

"What else should I do?" she asked, completely disconcerted.

"You will come to the wedding, I hope, Mam?" Tobin asked quietly, with a wink at his mother Bridget did not miss. It brought a smile to Mrs. Brennan's face, which was doubtless his intent.

"Of course, son."

"Would you be willing to come back with us? We are going to London."

"I cannot yet. I need time to consider."

Tobin scowled his disappointment. Bridget doubted he realized it.

His mother hastened to reassure him. "I will come for the wedding, son."

CHAPTER 16

$\mathcal{T}$obin and Bridget arrived back at Wrexford very late that night. It had been difficult to leave his mother there alone. He hoped he could convince her to live with them once they were married. He was surprised to find Wrexford still awake and waiting for them. Bridget excused herself to retire, but Wrexford wanted to talk. Tobin followed him into his study and accepted a glass of whisky before they sat down.

"How was your visit, son?"

"Successful, I think. I have both the birth certificate and the proof of my baptism. I could not convince her to return with us."

"I was secretly hoping she would come," Wrexford said, with obvious disappointment.

"You still care for her?" Tobin asked with surprise.

"How could I not?"

"I meant no offence. I suppose what your father did to you was difficult for both of you. I think Mam will come around, but you might need to woo her. She had not opened your letter until we arrived. She thought it was bad news about me from the war."

A look of pain crossed Wrexford's face. "I knew I should have gone in person. I was afraid she would refuse to see me."

Tobin was affected deep inside by his father's reaction. He really did care for his mother.

"Will she come for the wedding?"

"If there will be a wedding." Tobin shook his head, then sipped his drink.

"Do not lose heart, son. There have been many changes in Bridget's life. Be a support to her and things will work out as they should." His father drained his glass and then stood up.

"We both need to rest since we leave for London tomorrow." They said their good nights and Tobin fell asleep thinking he needed to take his own advice and woo Bridget. He had to convince her that nothing would change except being able to support her. That should be a strong point in his favour, not a mark against him, surely?

It seemed strange to be heading back to England so soon, but Tobin had not really planned any farther than seeing Bridget settled. He was still very angry on her behalf at the way her family had treated her. He knew they had been the ones to steal her money, but how could he prove it?

They were able to reach Portsmouth by late afternoon, due to a favourable easterly wind. There they took rooms for the evening and journeyed on to London the next day in a post chaise. Tobin hoped he would not have to travel again for some time. It was unpleasant being cramped in a small conveyance when he was used to the freedom of riding everywhere.

Bridget had said little the entire trip, and Tobin did not force her. He wished she would talk to him like she used to, though. He was not good at speaking about his feelings, choosing silence or sarcasm instead. He had learned to bottle up what bothered him, as if locking it away inside would make it go away. He did not know Bridget well enough to know if this was how she dealt with grief or if she was shutting him out because that was what she thought was best for him.

"Will you both stay at Wrexford House?" his father asked.

"I thought you would be more comfortable at Waverley Place, since you and the Duchess are friends," Tobin said to Bridget.

"Is that what you wish, my dear?" Wrexford asked her.

"I would prefer to go to my father's house. I still have many belongings there and as we are not married, I think it is for the best. We cannot go on in London as we have done elsewhere."

"That is certainly the case," Wrexford agreed, "although being betrothed allows more freedom. But you intend to go to the house alone?"

"I will have my maid, and our old retainers are still there. At least, I assume they are," she said with a frown. "Hopefully the solicitor did not dismiss them."

"May we set you down at your home, sir, and then I will see Bridget settled?" Tobin suggested.

"If that is your wish, my dear. There is plenty of room for you should you change your mind."

"Thank you for your many kindnesses to me, sir," Bridget said to Wrexford. Tobin climbed back into the carriage after they had let his father out on Bruton Street.

"Is this what you really want, lass?" Tobin asked as they rolled on to the town house Bridget had shared with her father and brother.

"I do not know what I want any more, except to rewind the clock a month and assassinate Napoleon before Waterloo began," she replied with a spark of fury.

"I wish I had thought to do that," Tobin agreed.

"I think some time alone will benefit both of us. I need to sort through Father's and Patrick's belongings and speak with a solicitor."

"I hope you do not mean to ignore me." He gave her a pointed look, which drew a small smile from her. "I do not think the Duchess will be pleased with you choosing to stay here alone. I do not like it myself, but I understand it."

"Thank you," she said and reached over and gave his hand a squeeze. "I do think I am safe from my relatives now, Tobin. It is not necessary for us to marry. Consider yourself free. I have no doubt, once you are the wealthy heir to the Wrexford title, you will have pretty ladies lining up to be courted."

"Is that supposed to entice me, *mo álainn*? I am tempted to kidnap you and drive on to Gretna."

"Do be serious, Tobin. I am trying to ease your conscience."

"Then ye are failing. I do not want to be free of ye." He looked at her, incredulous, his brogue slipping.

"If you are trying to hold me to everything I said when I thought you were unconscious, please forget it. Everything has changed since then." She crossed her arms and looked out of the window.

"Some things have changed, true enough... but only my being slightly more eligible. Besides, what would you do? How would you support yourself?"

"Must you ask such a thing? You know I have no answer to that until I speak with the solicitor."

"Please tell me you consider me a better choice than Riordan," he retorted.

"Do not even jest about that," she snapped.

"If you have changed your mind about me, then say so. I plan to use this time to woo you properly." What was going on here?

"I am in mourning."

"I was not suggesting anything inappropriate, unfortunately." He smiled devilishly.

The carriage stopped before they could argue further. Tobin could not believe how stubborn Bridget was being about this. He climbed down from the carriage, assisted Bridget to the pavement and with her maid following, walked his betrothed up the steps to the narrow stone house that stood five storeys high in a row of terraced homes.

Dusk had already fallen and the other homes had some sort of light in them, but this one had no knocker on the door and no other sign of inhabitance. Tobin did not have a good feeling about this, though with the master gone to war and two older retainers living there, perhaps they were simply at the back of the house. He knocked on the door and waited several minutes, but there was still no answer.

"Perhaps we should try the servant's entrance," Bridget suggested. "I do not think Mr. and Mrs. Brown would be expecting anyone."

"Do you have a key, lass?"

"No, perhaps there is one in my father's trunks. Wait, we did keep one in the flower box." She walked over to one of the first floor windows and felt beneath one of the boxes. She shook her head.

Tobin climbed down the iron-railed stone steps to the servants' and tradesmen's entrance. He knocked on the door there, but it was also complete darkness, and again, there was no answer.

"Perhaps they are gone away on holiday. I have not written to warn them to expect me, after all," Bridget reasoned.

"Either way, we must see you settled somewhere tonight. We can investigate on the morrow. Would you be more comfortable with the Duke and Duchess or at Wrexford's house?"

Bridget stared at him for a moment in disbelief. It did seem as though nothing was going right for her. "It matters little to me."

"Very well." He held out his hand to direct the ladies back into the carriage. Tobin thought Bridget would be more comfortable with another lady than in a bachelor house, although she had lived with her father and brother for some time. It seemed more proper, somehow, for her to be with the Duchess. Perhaps she would know how to bring some happiness back into Bridget's life.

It was only a few streets to Waverley Place. The butler recognized Tobin and admitted them immediately.

"Tobin!" the Duke and Duchess exclaimed as the butler announced them. Their Graces came across the room at once and welcomed them with open arms.

"We were not expecting to see you here, though you are very welcome," the Duchess said. "In fact, we were wondering when we would be summoned to Ireland for a wedding."

Tobin watched Bridget blush.

"I was just telling him there is no need for us to marry now. It seems he is to be his father's heir soon if not the heir to the title."

"That is incredible news, Tobin," the Duke said, looking as surprised as Tobin had felt when his father had first broken the news to him.

"Father has brought me here to parade me around in hopes of convincing the Members of Parliament that I am worthy to be a peer.

Bridget had hoped to stay at her family's house, but it was locked and none of the servants answered."

The Duke frowned. "When I last spoke to the Browns there was no plan for them to leave. We can speak to these solicitors tomorrow and see if they know anything."

"Thank you, I would appreciate that," Bridget said.

Tobin had agreed to return to Wrexford House and so, with reluctance, he left Bridget, promising to return the next day.

BRIDGET TRIED NOT to show her anxiety when her home had been locked up, but she knew something was wrong. Dungarvan had a hand in this, she knew—but could she prove it? And what could she do in the meantime? It was frustrating being a female at times. She highly doubted anyone would speak to her without a gentleman present. There had to be a way to get into her house. She would go back again tomorrow and try. Perhaps—no, hopefully—Waverley had missed something.

The next day, it was not too difficult to escape. The Duchess was distracted with her daughter in the nursery, and the Duke was from home. She even took her maid, Maria, with her for propriety's sake, though what her old nursemaid from Spain could do to protect her, Bridget was sure she did not know. Nonetheless, they were in London now, where all the rules were different. Not that she was greatly concerned with her reputation after the events of the last few weeks; she was not exactly a prime catch on the marriage mart.

No one answered the front door again when they arrived, and no one answered at the servant's entrance. Bridget had already decided to try the door from the mews if they found the house abandoned again. She had even bought a tool to pick the lock if she could make sense of how it worked.

Maria said little as they made their way around the row of houses to the back alley that led to the gardens. Fortunately, the gate latch was open and they were able to get as far as that without a struggle.

The flowers and beds looked well tended, and some ripe vegetables were plump and waiting to be picked.

"They cannot have been gone long." Maria said what Bridget was thinking. "Do you think maybe they went on holiday?"

"I hope it is something so simple. Father would not have cast them off. He would have provided for them in the will." *Where is it, though?* she asked herself.

They climbed down the steps to the door on the ground floor and it was locked as well. Bridget let out a sigh and pulled a jemmy from her reticule.

"Never tell me you mean to break in?" Maria asked in outrage.

"What choice do I have? I am the legal owner as next of kin," Bridget argued, though she wondered if she could still be arrested since nothing has been settled. Never before would she have considered such a thing, but she was desperate.

"I think you should leave this up to Mr. O'Neill and the Duke. They will make certain you do not go without." Maria continued to protest.

"You may wait at the front if you do not wish to help," Bridget snapped, losing patience with her long-time maid.

Tobin probably would have known how to do this, Bridget thought testily as she poked and jiggled and jammed the tools this way and that. The latch did not budge as she felt perspiration trickle down her back and under her bonnet. It was hard work, breaking and entering.

"The window is open, Miss Bridget," Maria said with some satisfaction, having waited nearby admiring Bridget's handiwork.

"Well met, Maria," Bridget said, tempted to give the maid a hug. "Give me a lift, will you? Then I will go in and undo the latch on the door for you."

Maria looked horrified, but was much too old and short to consider climbing in herself. Bridget shrugged. She had already lost her dignity that day.

Once inside, the house looked as though it had been abandoned in a hurry. There was food in the larder and a few dishes in the sink.

Bridget went on into the butler's and housekeeper's rooms on the same floor. A few personal effects and clothes were gone, according to Maria, but not everything.

"Perhaps they did go away for a short visit somewhere," Bridget said hopefully.

"It is not like Mrs. Brown to leave things untidy, though," Maria remarked.

"Let us go upstairs. I have little hope of finding anything since Waverley did not, but it is worth looking." Bridget took the first floor and Maria went to the second. At first, everything appeared normal, but when she entered her father's study, it had been ransacked. Pictures had been thrown off the walls, drawers were opened and papers scattered everywhere, and the carpets had been pulled up. Bridget stood still, looking around in disbelief before realizing she was trembling with fear.

"Miss Bridget!" Maria yelled from the floor above. "Come quickly! Someone has robbed the house!"

Bridget stepped out into the entrance hall and looked up. "Yes, I can see that down here as well. I believe we should go through the house together," Bridget suggested with surprising calm. She had a strong suspicion her cousin had been responsible for this. But what had he been looking for that Waverley would not have found?

Maria hurried back down the stairs. "I think we should go and fetch Mr. O'Neill. I do not feel safe here alone."

"We are not alone, Maria. We have each other. Besides, we broke in as well. I imagine Mr. and Mrs. Brown probably came home and found the house this way and left in a fright."

"Would they not have told someone? This does not make sense." The maid was frowning.

Bridget did not feel like explaining her cousin's motives at the moment and kept quiet. She walked through the entire house, looking at what had been ransacked but leaving things as they were. She agreed with Maria that she would like to bring Tobin and perhaps the Duke back, with the solicitors, to see what had been done.

Luckily, she found a key in Patrick's possessions and put it in her reticule so she would not have to break into what was rightfully hers. Some of her keepsakes were still in her bedroom, plus a few things she had inherited from her mother.

Besides the study, the most damage had been done to her father's bedchamber. Again, the pictures had been taken off the walls, possibly in a search for something hidden there. The mattress was overturned and all of the drawers had been emptied.

"What were they looking for, I wonder?" Bridget asked aloud. "If Riordan was looking for something here, then he must not have the will either." The few small jewels of her mother's were in Bridget's belongings back at Waverley Place. She frowned. Had Riordan found what he wanted—what she wanted? At least some kind of clue would be nice. A chill crept over her as she realized this disturbance very likely meant he was in London. He must be desperate indeed if he were stooping to such measures to make certain she did not find the will. Where would her father have kept it? Nothing made sense to Bridget any more. Her father was hardly a wealthy man!

The only room that appeared untouched was her mother's. Bridget could not stop herself from walking inside to capture the essence of her mother and the hint of rose water that still lingered there.

A small miniature of Mama with Father sat on the dressing table, along with a bottle of scent and her hairbrush. Bridget drew her finger across the surface, wishing she could have a few more moments with her mother. She would know what to do.

A few tears escaped down Bridget's cheek as grief and anger and a longing so painful she could hardly bear it wrenched at her insides. It would be easier to join them than suffer alone. She walked to the wardrobe which held a few of her mother's clothes that Bridget could not bear to part with. The smell of lavender used to keep the moths away rushed at her as the doors opened. Twenty-two years. How could she have been gone so long? In some ways it felt like yesterday, but in others not; it was hard to remember her voice. Soon, it would be like that with Father and Patrick. She could not help but wonder why had she been left behind as she tenderly fingered the blue silk gown, the tattered lace now yellowed. That had been her mother's wedding dress. Bridget used to dream of wearing it herself, one day. She swallowed a huge sob that escaped and wiped at her eyes with the back of her hand.

"Miss Bridget? I think someone is coming!" Maria whispered. Bridget was rooted to the spot for a second before hurrying quietly down the servants' stairs to try to see who dared, grabbing a Brown Bess from the boot room as she went. Her nerves were worn thin, and she had had enough of Riordan.

CHAPTER 17

*T*obin felt like a doll being played with by a little girl. In reality, he was first turned this way and that at London's finest tailor, Weston, and then his feet were scrutinized at its finest boot maker, Hoby. His father had made them both appointments to be outfitted in the latest fashions since they were presenting Tobin to Society. He kept reminding Wrexford that he was not a débutante just out of the schoolroom. Tobin even went so far as to mention he was still an officer in His Majesty's Army and had uniforms to wear when he went out and about. All of his protestations fell on deaf ears.

Tobin was only enduring this for Bridget, and she would not be attending most Society events due to her mourning. Thinking of his betrothed, he wondered what she was doing this morning. He would call at Waverley Place as soon as he was done with this nonsense.

He thought of Bridget and how sad she had looked. He wanted to bring a smile back to her beautiful face. Waverley had gone off to see his solicitor with his secretary. Tobin had intended to go as well, but Wrexford had thought his wardrobe a dire emergency. Tobin now looked at the man in question with growing affection. It surprised him, since he had perfected the art of hating him from the age of five.

Frankly, Bridget's stubbornness also surprised Tobin. She had been so open about their friendship and wanting to marry him before. As a gentleman's daughter, she was more than an eligible match for him. Was there more to her change of heart than that weak excuse? He hated the direction of his thoughts.

Then he was dragged off to White's Gentlemen's Club, the likes of whose doors Tobin had never thought to darken. Wrexford proceeded to introduce him to all his cronies and they were invited to have a light luncheon with them. Tobin was trying to be polite, but his mind was elsewhere. He was unused to gentlemanly ways. He preferred to be busy.

Many of the gentlemen wished to hear details of Waterloo; it was still something of a fantastical story to many of them. Tobin told some abbreviated tales to a captive audience before they thankfully moved on to the grouse hunting to be had in Scotland. All Tobin could think about was Bridget and how upset she had been last night.

"Why are you scowling, son?" Wrexford asked.

Tobin looked up. "I beg your pardon. I am worried about Bridget."

Wrexford laughed and spoke to his friends. "He has not been away from his betrothed for twelve hours and he is already pining for her. She is quite a pretty thing, I confess. My son has done well for himself."

The men all laughed and ribbed him good-naturedly about young love.

Tobin left with an extra spring in his step, and stopped to purchase some flowers for her from the seller on the corner. It was a little ridiculous how excited he was to see Bridget. However, when he arrived at Waverley Place, he was disappointed to find Bridget had gone out. However, the Duke had returned from seeing the solicitor and was in his study, Timmons informed him.

"Excellent. Thank you, Timmons. I will show myself in."

Tobin knocked on the door even though it was open. The Duke looked up. "Tobin, come on in. You know you have no need for formality here. You look exhausted."

"I would rather move camp than go shopping on Bond Street, any day."

Waverley chuckled. "Poor Tobin. Help yourself to a drink and have a seat. Is something amiss?"

"Nothing other than Wrexford insisting I be decked out like a bloody Tulip."

Waverley laughed and then laughed some more. He only stopped when Tobin glared at him.

"Did you not mention you are still in the army?"

"He thinks I will sell out. I have not made up my mind on that yet. Where is Miss Murphy?"

"She only told Meg she had some business to attend to, but that was early this morning. She took her maid with her."

Tobin frowned. Her maid was but a small, elderly Spanish lady. "What did the solicitor have to say?"

"He had no knowledge of the house being shut up or the servants being sent away. He did not see any difficulty in Miss Murphy inhabiting the house until the court ruling."

"Something is not right, and she cannot stay there with only her maid," Tobin remarked.

"I agree, so I put Jamison on it." Jamison was the Duke's London man of business and could ferret out a rat from the bowels of London's sewers faster than a flood.

"Perhaps we should go and look over the house. Do you think she could have gone back there?" Tobin continued to worry.

"I am sure I could not say, but it seems a reasonable place to start. I still have the key from when I went before. I forgot to give it back to the Browns."

Waverley sent word to the Duchess and then the men were on their way. They walked since it was only a few streets away and it was a beautiful day.

Waverley knocked at the front door and there was no answer.

"Perhaps I was mistaken," Tobin said.

The Duke took out the key. "Should we check and see if anything is wrong? Just to satisfy Miss Murphy?"

"I suppose it cannot hurt," Tobin agreed. Waverley unlocked the door and allowed Tobin to enter first. The first thing he saw was the barrel of a gun pointed at him. On instinct, he lurched at Waverley to protect him as a loud boom shook the house.

"Tobin!" Bridget screamed from somewhere through a fog in his brain. Suddenly he was in the middle of a battle, deep in a muddy trench with heavy smoke and the sound of muskets and cannon sounding all around him.

Someone was shaking him and holding him down and he began to fight back, kicking and punching.

"Tobin!" A familiar voice sounded.

"Get down, your Grace!" he shouted back as he felt around for his own rifle. It must be somewhere nearby. He was struggling for breath and sweat was pouring into his eyes.

Then a gush of cold water poured over him. He opened his eyes, blinking, and stared into the faces of Bridget and the Duke.

"What happened"? he asked, somewhat embarrassed to be lying on the floor in a strange place, drenched with water.

"My gun misfired, and thankfully hit the wall instead of you," Bridget said meekly. "Are you harmed? I am so terribly sorry!"

"I thought we were back at Cuidad Rodrigo. The Frogs were shooting at us," he explained as he tried to get his bearings and calm his breathing.

Bridget sat back on the floor and put her hands to her eyes. She was crying.

"I thought you were Riordan. The house has been ransacked."

Tobin sat up and put his arms around her. "Fret not, lass. I know you did not mean to do it. Sometimes I have nightmares where I am back in the heat of a fire-fight. I expect the sound of the gun startled me."

She was nodding. "It sometimes happened to Papa and Patrick, too. I could have killed you!"

"Hush, lass. Everything is well," he whispered as he rocked her. He noticed Waverley and the maid leave discreetly. "You said the house had been ransacked? Do you think it was your cousin?"

"Who else could it have been? The main damage was in Father's study and his chambers. He must have been looking for the will.

There are no jewels to be found here. There are few enough of those in my jewellery box at Waverley Place."

"And there is no sign of your butler or housekeeper?"

"No." She shook her head. "It does look as though they left in a hurry. Perhaps the intruder startled them. That is why I think it was Rory. He might have known there was a spare key in the flower pot. Not that it is a great hiding place. It was there for Patrick when he came home late."

Tobin stood up and helped her to her feet.

"Have you been searching through everything? Is anything missing?"

"Not that I can see. I should straighten everything back as it should be. Perhaps, if I take Father's papers with me, I might find something to help."

"Waverley mentioned his man of business was trying to see if the general had a solicitor here in London. It is a common practice, apparently. Jamison discovered your dowry account had been emptied."

"I cannot believe it was Father or Patrick. In Father's last conversation with me, he made a point of saying I had been provided for."

"They both loved you dearly, lass. It was not they," Tobin said as he helped her gather the papers and set the study back to rights. Waverley and the maid came back downstairs.

"We have straightened the general's chamber," Waverley said. "Have you found anything in here?"

"Nothing other than a lot of accounts and letters. Bridget wants to take them back to sort through them. I just need to replace the pictures and drawers and we can leave."

Waverley and Maria began to help them straighten the study. Bridget sat down at the desk, stacking the papers and placing them into a satchel. Tobin replaced the drawers and as he jostled the last one, a false bottom opened up.

Bridget gasped. "I thought those only existed in novels. Is anything inside?"

Tobin felt around, fearing she was to be disappointed until his finger caught on a small piece of paper and he pulled it out.

"I do not think this is a will," he said as he handed it to her.

"No," she agreed. "But there is a name of a solicitor."

THAT NIGHT, the Duchess had invited Wrexford and Tobin to dine with them. Bridget was still having great difficulty reconciling the fact that she had shot at Tobin and sent him into a horrible panic. How could she have mistaken Tobin for Riordan?

Wrexford and the Duke and Duchess were conversing amiably about Tobin's possibility of becoming the heir, but Tobin was very quiet as the servants placed the food *à la français* on the table so they could serve themselves.

"What is wrong, Tobin?" Bridget asked.

"I feel like a fish out of water," he admitted.

"You do not have to do any of this," she assured him, taking his hand under the table and giving it a squeeze.

"I do," he argued.

"I would be perfectly happy to return to the army when you are convalesced. We do not have to make any other decisions now."

He glanced at her gratefully. "If you agree to marry me," he reminded her in a dry tone.

"Yes, if I agree to marry you." She wanted nothing more, but was becoming more and more certain it was the wrong thing to do. "You can always return to the army, with or without me."

They both turned their heads as Wrexford spoke up. "Parliament will hear your case this session, before they dismiss for the summer, after all."

"That is excellent news," the Duchess said. "Do you foresee any problems?"

"Not since we have the certificate of birth, and my marriage certificate to my other marriage. It proves Tobin was born before the annulment was granted."

Bridget's heart sank. Selfishly, she had hoped to keep Tobin as he was.

"I was able to present Tobin to many of the voting members today, and I think they are all satisfied he is competent to fulfil the position." Wrexford beamed.

"Of course he is," the Duchess agreed.

"I would like to plan a ball to celebrate the return of my son into my life," Wrexford announced. "Even if they do not decide to make him my legitimate heir, he will inherit everything else unentailed."

"I think it is an excellent idea," Waverley agreed.

"May we host it here?" the Duchess asked.

"That would be splendid," the Duke agreed. "If you are amenable, Wrexford. I owe Tobin much, and it would bring us great pleasure."

"Bridget is in mourning, your Grace," Tobin protested, but Bridget put her hand on his arm.

"That is no reason not to celebrate your being reunited with your father. Please do not refuse on my account." Not that Wrexford would allow it, she thought with a wry twist of her lips.

"As long as I can make it known I am betrothed to you," Tobin agreed, though with much reluctance. Bridget knew he did not enjoy balls and other such amusements, but it was to be his future.

Bridget did not answer.

"We must make haste if we are to hold the ball before everyone leaves Town," the Duchess added.

"My secretary is equal to the task, I have no doubt," Waverley replied.

"Then I shall consult our invitations and see what day is available," the Duchess remarked.

Bridget excused herself as soon as was polite after dinner and tea. There was much to think about and do. Sorting through her father's papers was a start, although she had little hope in that quarter. The solicitor, however, was more promising. Waverley had already given the name to his secretary to investigate, but Bridget felt time was running out, especially if Riordan was searching for the same thing she was.

The next morning, Bridget sent Maria out to buy the morning papers. She did not wish to ask for the Duke's copies because she knew her reasons would be objectionable to them. Maria was then to go to the agencies and enquire about positions for her, but the maid voiced her displeasure and refused quite categorically. Unfortunately, there was nothing Bridget was really qualified for except nursing. Would any of the hospitals hire her to do such a thing? Surely there were a great number of wounded and injured who had been brought back from Waterloo and needed care, but how could she convince someone to hire her? A lady did not work except for genteel employment as a governess or companion. Besides, anyone who could recommend her was currently in France with the army.

Bridget began to pace around the room with frustration. She wanted to visit the solicitor, but knew she should wait for the Duke's man to do so. He would get much further than she. Bridget stopped then, when she had an idea. She rang for her maid.

"Maria, please fetch my bonnet and pelisse. We are going out."

Maria glowered. "Where to now?"

"We are going to visit the soldiers at the infirmary."

A look of resignation crossed the maid's face. "I will join you downstairs."

There had to be someone wounded she knew. Visiting would give her a reason to be there.

Soon they were on their way to St. Bartholomew's in a hackney cab. Bridget felt guilty, as though she were sneaking about behind Tobin's back, but it was necessary. Besides, she genuinely did wish to visit the wounded soldiers who were recovering.

The smell of carbolic mixed with gangrenous wounds was like walking into a steaming sewer when they entered St. Bart's. Maria could not stomach it, so she elected to wait outside. Bridget could not blame her. She had expected it, yet it was horrifying. Breathing through her mouth did not fully mask the odour.

No one took any notice of her presence, so she marched into the ward and began speaking to each of the patients who were awake. It was something she had always done in the camp hospital. There were never enough orderlies for all the work. She straightened pillows, she gave sips of water, changed bandages, and she even held a basin while someone retched. It was somehow comforting to do those things she had done before. Yet nowhere did she see any female attendants or patients.

One voice called out to her. "Miss Murphy?"

"Sergeant Jones," she said, turning with a smile to a man who was missing both legs.

"How do you do?" she asked.

"I am alive, and that is something," he answered. "It is nice to see a pretty face for a change."

She smiled at him, always humbled when someone with dire injuries could maintain a positive outlook. "Who are the surgeons attending here?"

"Dr. Wheeler was the last I saw. He came back on the packet with us."

"I know him well," she said. "I will try to find him. Do you need anything, Sergeant?"

"I am hoping to leave here in a day or two. All I want is to go home to Yorkshire to see my missus."

"Then I will wish you a safe journey," she said. Bridget moved on to the ward upstairs where she found Dr. Wheeler extracting some shrapnel from a patient. "I had not expected to see you so soon, sir," she said, coming to stand beside him at the bed.

"Well, I'll be, Miss Murphy. What are you doing in London, lass? I thought you were off to Ireland."

"I was there. It is a very long story. You would not happen to need help here, would you?"

"That is the silliest question I have ever heard from you. We always need more hands."

"I am relieved to hear it, because I need a position," she said, deciding to be candid.

Dr. Wheeler looked up at her, frowning. "This is no place for you to be employed, lass. It is not a camp hospital. There are no female attendants to my knowledge."

Yet she was acceptable as a volunteer? "Perhaps we could change that," she said softly.

He stared at her for a moment and then sighed. "I will see what I can do. I thought your father would have left you provided for."

"He thought he did," she answered. There was really nothing else to say. "I will come back here tomorrow."

CHAPTER 18

a ball? In his honour? Tobin shook his head. The Duchess had announced it only five days ago, that being the one evening without any major conflicts before the *ton* departed en masse for the country. It was too much to be borne, especially if Bridget could not attend.

Tobin had not seen Bridget in those five days. Every day he had called, but she had been out visiting the sick, the Duchess said. That she would seek out the wounded soldiers surprised him not at all, but he had a sneaking suspicion she was avoiding him. She had not been dining with the family. Jamison had been busy with preparations for the ball so had not yet visited the solicitor.

Today was the ball, where he was to be paraded before the *beau monde*. He could not wait to have the agonies over and done. Somehow, he was more nervous than he had been before his first battle.

Wrexford's appeal had been approved by Parliament, he had informed him before leaving on some important errand. Tobin wanted to tell Bridget himself. Only she would understand his feelings. Hopefully, now she would have no more reservations about marrying and he could talk her out of her silly notions about setting him free. He was now a viscount, of all things—even if it was a courtesy title—and the heir to a wealthy earldom. Over the past week, his father had been tutoring him on estate management and his responsibilities. Tobin's head felt as if it would explode with the knowledge, not to mention the shrapnel damage. He prayed fervently that Wrexford lived to be a hundred. How was he to survive an entire ball as the guest of honour if he could not slink back into the corner... or have Bridget by his side?

He donned his dress regimentals, the blue of the Guards, wondering if he would go back. If it was the only way to woo her, he would do it. Bridget's absence had made it impossible to court her properly but he had an idea, even though she might kill him for it later.

He arrived early at Waverley Place and the family was upstairs, finishing their ablutions, and the servants were downstairs, taking an early dinner, so Tobin walked through the surprisingly quiet house. The ballroom doors were flung open, as were the terrace doors, to let what little breeze existed flow through the house. The wooden floor was polished to a high shine and the room has been transformed into an inside garden. Greenery and red roses covered every available surface and filled every pot. The mirrored wall opposite the doors magnified the effect. Soon the candles would be lit and they would make the room appear bathed in sunshine. *This is all for me.* He shook his head, still disbelieving his change in circumstances. However, there was one constant: he wanted none of it if Bridget would not be by his side.

Was she upstairs, dressing? He was told she would be present at the formal dinner but not the ball. It was only appropriate, he supposed, but he did not like it.

Reasoning with himself that he would have no other opportunity for private conversation with her, he made his way upstairs to the door of her chambers. He knocked lightly and heard her voice bid him enter.

She was sitting on a pale blue chaise longue next to the window, looking out over the rear gardens. She did not turn her head to look at him. Few people could look as beautiful as she in mourning, but it only accentuated her porcelain skin and ebony hair. She wore an evening gown of a high-waisted, fashionable style but in unrelieved black. There was no jewellery adorning her neck or ears. Tobin admired her elegant profile and thought she deserved to be a lady in truth. He could finally give that to her, but he could not fathom doing it for anyone else. He waited for her to turn and notice him. That it took a few minutes was an attestation to her distraction. What was on her mind?

Her head turned and she smiled sadly, as though she had been contemplating something distasteful.

"Tobin."

He walked into the room, closing the door behind him. Propriety be hanged. "I brought these for you." He held out some gardenias to her. He could not see or walk by them without thinking of her scent.

She took them and held them to her nose. "Thank you. That is thoughtful of you."

"I would have brought you a nosegay, but I did not think you could wear it."

She shook her head. "I heard the news… my lord."

Her dark blue eyes looked up and the anguish he saw there hurt him more than any of the wounds he had on his body.

"*Mo grá.*" He went down on his knees before her and took her hands in his without thought for any creases he might be placing in his uniform. "What is it?"

She searched his face and ran her fingers down his cheek. "It is nothing. I am pleased for you."

"Bugger me. I want you to be happy for us."

She swallowed hard and he had a sinking feeling, but the gong sounded for dinner and there was no more time to finish pouring his heart out to her.

"May we speak later? I have many things I wish to say."

She took his hand but did not answer. He walked her downstairs to the drawing room, where a few guests waited who had been invited to the formal dinner before the ball.

"Mam!" he said with boyish excitement as he saw his mother,

looking like the lady she was born to be, dressed in a beautiful blue gown that made her look twenty years younger. Of course, she was a beautiful woman. Her smile lit up her face. She was on his father's arm and Wrexford was looking down at her with such tenderness that Tobin felt his throat tighten. He walked towards them and kissed her on the cheek. "You came."

"I promised I would," she answered with a twinkle in her eye.

"You promised you would come for the wedding."

"So I did." His mother looked towards Bridget and her eyes narrowed a little with apparent concern.

"Miss Murphy." His mother curtsied.

Bridget returned the courtesy. "Mrs. Brennan."

"Lady Wrexford," Lord Wrexford corrected.

"My felicitations," Bridget said, clearly distracted. "If you will excuse me, I see someone I need to speak with."

"Is something the matter, son?" his mother asked softly as they watched Bridget walk over to the Duke and Duchess.

"I wish I knew, Mam. I do not think she is happy about all of this."

His mother's hand was on his arm. "Be patient with her, she has lost much and I can certainly understand how this would be overwhelming." She looked over her shoulder to where Wrexford was now conversing with someone else and lowered her voice. "I do not know if I will ever become used to being called Lady Wrexford after all this time."

"He looks at you as though he adores you," Tobin remarked. "Are you certain you wish to do this?"

"It is a little late for regrets now, dearest, and I would do anything for you. However, he has been everything that is gracious and perhaps it will be pleasant, even at my age."

"He has certainly tried to make up for lost time with me," Tobin admitted, surprising himself. "I only hope I have not gained one family only to lose another."

"You love her," his mother stated.

"Of course I do."

"Then fight for her, son," Wrexford said behind his ear. "Do not be a coward like I was."

Wrexford's words echoed in his ear all through dinner and after. Something was going on, and Tobin had to determine what it was before it was too late. This had to be resolved, and he knew he needed Jamison's help.

~

BRIDGET SAT through dinner going through the motions and forcing smiles, although her heart was heavy. She listened to the news about Tobin until she lost her appetite, even though she was delighted for Tobin and his reunited family.

"Tobin was born before the annulment. Everyone seemed to think the request reasonable since I am the last in the line. It did not hurt, either, that Wellington and Waverley spoke up on his behalf." Lord Wrexford beamed and raised his glass to the Duke.

If it was not that, then others were hinting about an upcoming wedding. Bridget had finally obtained an audience with her father's solicitor the day prior. She would have the town house, which might sell for a thousand pounds, but her dowry was gone. He apologised profusely, but could not explain how or to where it had disappeared since the bank had released the funds. Without any income, Bridget could not afford to keep the house. She might be able to purchase a small cottage somewhere in the country and live off of the percents, but the fact was, she was poor. Dr. Wheeler had found her a private nursing position, but it would require moving to Norfolk and giving up Maria.

After dinner, Bridget slipped away while the rest of the extended family went to greet the *ton* arrivals in a receiving line. Bridget could see everything from the floor above. Potted palms and flowers decorated even this hidden alcove and the matching one at the other end where the musicians prepared to play. The Duchess had told her about the secret alcove if she wished to observe or listen.

Bridget did not wish, really, but she could not seem to stay away.

Everything was ready for her departure, including a letter to Tobin. It had taken her hours to write it after starting afresh five times. The cream of Society filed through the doors for well over an hour before the dancing began, all seemingly eager to welcome this long-lost son into their bosom. What Bridget would not give to have Tobin watching this with her and exchanging derogatory remarks about the fickle nature of Society! From illegitimate and poor to a wealthy heir —it was too much to absorb. Those who would not have acknowledged him on the street a month ago were now throwing their daughters in his path. No doubt Tobin was miserable now, but he would adjust to his new position in time, and with some lady bred to it. Much though Bridget would like to pretend she was up to the task, neither she nor Tobin were, and now she had nothing to bring to the marriage.

Tobin looked magnificent in his dress regimentals. Besides his height, he filled out every inch to perfection, and his dark hair and green eyes stood out even from here. He was not the only one in uniform, but all others paled in comparison to him. Bridget watched as lady after lady was introduced to Lord Kilmorgan, many blatant in their assessments and approvals. Tobin was now one of the most eligible bachelors, and the mamas wanted an advantage over those who had been so unfortunate to leave early for the country.

The musicians struck up a tune and the ball began. Beautiful gowns in a rainbow of colours twirled around the room in cadence with the tunes. Bridget thought back to her first dance with Tobin, the one Patrick had orchestrated. Tobin's charm and devilish grin had ensnared her from the first moment. When she thought back to how bold she had been with him, she almost could not believe it. If only things could go back to the way they were before. A tear dropped from her eye and she wiped it away. He was so very dear.

Her hiding spot was like an echo chamber, with voices wafting straight to her ears.

Three women gossiped openly; there was no surprise there.

"He is a taking thing, though I always have been soft for a man in uniform."

"I heard they are all Catholic."

"No, no, you have it all wrong. That is why the marriage was annulled in the first place. I heard Lord and Lady Wrexford had to remarry in the Anglican Church to make this all valid again."

"So this makes the second marriage and the dead Kilmorgan illegitimate."

"Apparently, but they are not alive to care, now, are they?"

Bridget heard that conversation more than once.

"Here he comes; smile, you look a fright. You must engage him to dance," a conniving mother warned.

"I heard he is not dancing, Mama. He has war injuries," the daughter added dreamily.

"Then you must find a way, Harriet," the mother scolded. Bridget felt sorry for the girl who looked very young in her white ruffles.

Bridget had not known Tobin was not dancing. Was his leg paining him? She leaned forward a little to try and get a glimpse of him, but instead her heart clenched when she saw Riordan enter the ballroom. It was very late and she knew he was not invited. What was he doing here?

He was very handsome in his black evening wear, including a pale green waistcoat. He was almost as handsome as Tobin, but she was biased. Even Bridget had to acknowledge Riordan turned heads. She was quite tempted to jump over the banister and strangle him until he told her where her money was.

He was looking around and people had taken notice of him. So had Tobin. He approached Riordan where he stood, a few steps higher than the ballroom. The two of them, standing next to each other, were nothing short of splendid. The young ladies giggled and simpered while the older ladies waved their fans and whispered to each other.

Bridget realized she was holding her breath and let it out. She had to think quickly. Could her cousin still be harbouring delusions that she would marry him? Or did he mean to take her by force? She frowned and sat down. Perhaps it was best just to confront her cousin. She noticed he wore a black arm band, but that did not prevent him from attending a ball.

Bridget should have left earlier. She had meant to be gone before the ball started. Escaping amongst the crowd entering would have been easy. Now, however, she needed to know what her cousin had done—if he would have the courage to tell her to her face.

She climbed down the narrow, spiral staircase to the floor below, and found she was in the servants' hall behind the ballroom. Pausing, she pondered how she could get her cousin's attention in order to speak with him alone. Tobin was likely to throw him out if he had his way.

Bridget hurried around to the front entrance and waited in the shadows. If he was looking for her to be dancing, he would be disappointed.

It was not long until the Duke and Tobin exited the ballroom, one on either side of her cousin. She did not want them to see her. It would only make things more difficult.

"I will leave on my own," Dungarvan said, holding his hands up. "There is no need to throw me out bodily. I only came to beg my cousin's forgiveness."

"I will pass on your apologies, but you would do better to return what is rightfully hers," Tobin growled.

"I do not know what you mean." Riordan proclaimed innocence.

"You mean for us to believe you did not steal her inheritance?"

"Why would I do that when I want to marry her? Besides, I learned only recently of my uncle's death!"

Somehow, Bridget believed him, though he could have borrowed on the assumption.

"We shall see," Waverley said. "We will call on you tomorrow and discuss this further. Now we must return to our guests."

Riordan gave a curt nod of his head and straightened his coat before walking out. There was only a small audience within earshot, but no doubt every word would be repeated in tomorrow's drawing rooms.

After Waverley and Tobin had gone back into the ballroom, Bridget escaped through the front door. Her cousin was walking at a fast pace, no doubt due to anger or humiliation, and Bridget almost had to run to catch up to him.

"Rory!" she called breathlessly.

"Bridget?" He turned, surprise clear upon his face and in his stance.

"You wished to speak with me?"

Riordan glanced around. "I did." He looked sheepish, like the boy who had been her playmate years ago. "I had hoped to convince you to reconsider my offer. I must humbly apologize for the circumstances in which we parted in Ireland."

He seemed sincere. Bridget was still cautious and needed him to say it to her face. "I can forgive you for that, but Rory, why did you steal my inheritance? It was what I was counting on to live."

He frowned. "I have done nothing of the sort."

"Then why are all Father's accounts, including the one containing my dowry, empty?"

"I have no idea." He held out his hands. "Do you think I would do that to you? I may be a bit under the hatches, but nothing to warrant theft. I truly thought you would wish to marry me and you know how Mama can be."

"I am surprised she allowed you to leave."

"Only under the condition that I bring back a bride. When I arrived, I heard you were not yet married, and I thought to try again without Mama's interference."

Bridget was more confused than ever. Would it be so horrible to be married to Rory if his mother were gone? It would have to be a white marriage, though, which is more than she would ever have if she went into service. For some reason she believed Rory had not taken her money.

She closed her eyes and made a decision. "If we were to marry, would you let me live independently? You would keep your properties, would you not?"

"We get along well, cousin. Why not live in the luxury of Dungarvan House?"

"I do not think I could bear my aunt's company, and frankly, I could not look the other way when you took lovers. It would be best to start as we mean to go on."

Riordan stared at her, his expression thoughtful as he evidently considered her offer.

"What about your lieutenant?"

"He no longer needs me, as you can see," she answered quietly. "You could look much higher in a bride yourself."

"Do not sell yourself short, cousin."

"I have no dowry, and I am the impoverished daughter of the second son of a baron."

"And you were far above his touch before," he argued, far too astutely for her comfort.

"Are you really trying to dissuade me now, when before you held me at gunpoint?"

Riordan inclined his head. "The previous proposal was not well done of me. I did not know the whole of the story and Mother was threatening me. I believe it is all sorted now."

Bridget was not so sure her aunt could ever be sorted.

"You love him," Riordan said softly, looking into her eyes.

"What would you have done for the one you loved?"

He looked away, not prepared for the question.

"I will meet you in the mews in half an hour. I must send someone a note." She would have to let Dr. Wheeler know she would not be taking the position. If only she could be certain this would be a better fate.

CHAPTER 19

hen Tobin saw Dungarvan, he had wanted to draw his cork right there in front of the entire *ton*. That would show them how refined he really was, he had thought with pleasurable malice. Mincing around a ballroom and smiling at young girls with spots was not Tobin's place in life. If Waverley had not held him back, Dungarvan would be spouting blood all over the ballroom floor at this very minute.

It was fortunate for him that Tobin needed to see Bridget. Thankfully, she would have no idea her cousin had come, and Tobin had to convince her to come downstairs for his announcement. He intended to do it after the supper dance, when his father introduced him as his heir.

Bridget would kill him, he thought with a grin as he mounted the stairs to knock on her chamber door. He waited expectantly but there was no answer. Could she have fallen asleep? It was hard to fathom how she might with the noise from the ballroom, but she had looked exhausted earlier, at dinner. He found the door unlocked and opened it to peer inside. There was no light burning in the sitting room, so he took one of the tapers waiting for guests and lit it from one of the sconces. Her bedroom was also dark and he held the light up over her bed. It was still made up. Where could she be? Was she watching the ball? Perhaps she was in the small alcove above the ballroom. Even he knew of it from his days as Waverley's man. He had little time to search because, as the guest of honour, he would be missed. He held the taper aloft to exit the room and a piece of parchment caught his eye. He leaned closer and saw his name scrolled across the back.

He cursed profusely and tore open the seal.

Dearest Tobin,

This is the hardest thing I have ever had to do, but in time, you will see that I have made the right decision. The time we had together is more precious than riches to me, and I will carry the memories of our friendship with me like treasures. Please do not worry or come after me out of honour. I will have the funds from the sale of the house and Maria and I will set up a household in the country somewhere. Find someone who can be your helpmeet in this new life of yours. But most importantly, be happy.

All my love,
Bridget

He ran down the stairs back to the ballroom and searched for the Duke and Duchess. They were waltzing. Of course, they would be when he needed them most. Where could she have gone? He racked his brain while he waited for the dance to end. Back to her family's house? Would she have gone there with only her maid? It was worth a try. She could have been gone for hours by now! The maid! Most likely, Bridget would have taken her wherever she went, but Tobin found a footman and asked him to see if Maria was in the house. If she was, he wanted to speak with her immediately. Maids always knew what their mistresses were about.

The Duke and Duchess finished their dance before the footman returned. Although Tobin pulled them aside, he had to wait to show them the letter until the guests had gone into the supper room.

They read the letter together.

"Why would she do this?" the Duke asked.

"Now things are beginning to make sense. She asked me to find her maid a position here. She said she was too old to see to her needs any more. Of course, I agreed," the Duchess added. "We must go into supper now for your father to make his announcement. We cannot let it be seen that anything is wrong. I will have Jamison and Timmons investigate to see what they can find out."

"I have already asked one of the footmen to send for her maid," Tobin said, feeling his scowl deepen.

"Escort my Duchess into the supper room as though nothing is wrong. I will meet you in my study once you can discreetly get away."

Tobin wanted to scream with impatience. Instead, he had to smile and nod and act like a jolly fool as several toasts were made to him, his title, his parents and on and on.

When he was finally able to escape to the study, trying not to run, he was champing at the bit with anxiety. Every possibility imaginable was going through his mind, but Lord Dungarvan had just been in the house. Was that a coincidence?

Maria was sitting on the edge of a chair, sniffing and dabbing her red eyes with a handkerchief.

"Anything?" Tobin asked as he entered the room and closed the door behind him.

Waverley pointed his hand in the direction of the maid. "Maria says Miss Murphy had taken a private nursing position in Norfolk."

"But—but she could not take me with her," the maid sobbed.

Tobin counted to ten. God save him from overwrought females! "Did she leave tonight?"

She nodded. "On the common stage!"

"When did she leave?"

"Half an hour past," she answered.

Waverley looked at Jamison. "Find out which stage-coach and what time." The secretary nodded and left the room.

Tobin paced up and down fast enough to wear a hole in the carpet. Waverley handed him a drink.

"Calm yourself. You need to have your wits to find her."

The butler entered, causing all of them to look up. Waverley opened it himself. It was Timmons with one of the footmen.

"Speak, Thomas," the butler demanded.

"I saw Miss Murphy leave through the front doors right after you threw Lord Dungarvan out, your Grace."

A string of Gaelic profanities escaped Tobin's lips and he did not care.

"Did she come back?" Waverley asked.

"I could not say, your Grace."

"Thank you, Thomas. If you think of anything else, please let us know immediately."

The footman bowed and left.

"There is something else, your Grace. Miss Murphy asked me to have this delivered." Timmons handed the Duke a letter addressed to a Dr. Wheeler.

Waverley took the note. "Did she leave after that?"

"No, she returned upstairs."

"Thank you, Timmons."

"Dr. Wheeler is one of the army surgeons, is he not?" Waverley asked. "He attended you in Brussels."

"It is possible," Tobin answered. "I was not awake for much of that time."

Maria blew her nose violently. "He is the one who arranged the position for her in Norfolk. She was visiting with him at St. Bartholomew's."

Waverley opened the note and read what appeared to be a hasty scrawl.

Dear Dr. Wheeler,

I will not be needing the position after all. Thank you for your kindness and willingness to help me. Godspeed in your future endeavours and I hope we will meet again under better circumstances.

Your fond servant,

Miss Bridget Murphy

"*Mallachdan.* I am going to kill Dungarvan when I find him."

"Easy, Tobin. Perhaps she came to her senses. I will have Jamison make certain she does not board the stage, but it does not seem likely that is where she went. Timmons, see if you may discover whether Dungarvan has a house here or where his rooms might be, will you?"

"I will go and ask Wrexford. He has some acquaintance with the family." The ball was almost ended as the last set was playing, thank God. It took Tobin a few minutes to make his way through the remaining crowd to his father and mother. People were only wanting to congratulate him and wish him well, but he wished it was for a different reason entirely.

"Tobin, there you are," his mother said with a smile.

"What is wrong, son?" Wrexford was frowning.

"Bridget has left and we do not know where she is. We think she may have gone with Dungarvan, either with or without her consent. I could not say which. Do you know if he has a house in Town?" Tobin asked as quietly as he could.

"Yes, I have dined there with his father before. 'Tis at the south end of Albermarle Street."

"Please make my excuses to the guests. I must go after her before she does something we will both regret."

"We will say our farewells with the Duchess," his father assured him. "Thankfully, most of the guests have already taken their leave."

Tobin took a back way through the servants' quarters on his return to avoid being turned from his purpose. He was out of breath when he reached the study.

"Albermarle Street. I have already sent for the carriage."

BRIDGET WAS TRYING NOT to dwell on second thoughts as she and Riordan made their way across Mayfair. He had come back for her with a hackney and loaded her trunks in the back alley like a fugitive, except no one would notice she was gone until morning. Reminding herself that this had been her choice—that it was best for Tobin—kept her from jumping from the moving vehicle.

Bridget was exhausted and she realized a fair amount of time had passed before she looked out of the window. Nothing was familiar.

"Why are we not stopping?"

Riordan gave a little shrug which she could barely detect by the light of the moon. "I decided we might as well get a start on our journey home. There is no need to delay now. It saves me the bother of opening the house."

"But I thought I could stay here after..." Why she was so stunned and angry, she could not say. "You said I could be independent. The marriage is only so you can retain the unentailed properties and I can be alone."

"Dearest cousin..." He shook his head in amusement. "There are certain appearances to maintain, and Mother would be devastated were we not to have a grand wedding."

"I cannot! You know I am in mourning!"

He gave her a pitying look.

"Let me out, now, Rory," she demanded.

"Bridget." His voice no longer implied the bored, lazy wastrel.

"This is a mistake. I do not know what I was thinking, but I cannot marry you!" She began to panic as she realized he had no intention of adhering to their agreement.

He sighed heavily. "I am afraid you leave me little choice."

"What do you mean?" she asked before he moved over to her side and grabbed her hands. The expression on his face at once made her begin to fear him.

"You truly have no idea, do you?" Barking a derisive laugh and holding her hands too tightly, he shook his head. "We must make a minor detour now, and I must make certain you do not try to escape."

Her eyes widened with fear as he pulled a piece of rope from a satchel at his feet. Immediately, she began to fight him, flailing her arms and kicking out wildly. Her boot connected with a shin and he let out a yelp of pain.

"Do not make me hurt you, cousin," he growled. "If there were any other way…" His voice trailed off before he completed his sentence, "…but there is not." He thrust her over onto her stomach and pulled her hands behind her back, tying them up so tightly she could scarcely breathe. He turned her over and set her back upright. "Do try to be comfortable. I will not be long."

She glared at him. "You do realize I have to consent to the marriage?"

"Ideally," he replied, before he stepped down from the carriage.

After she heard his footsteps recede, she shuffled over to the window to try to see if there was any hope of escape. All she could see was darkness with the blackened expanse of a deep wood in the distance. They must be far from the city already, she realized, trying not to panic. She lifted her foot to the handle of the door, but she could not get adequate power to force it open. She fell to her knees and tried her mouth with more success. Unfortunately, the pressure required to push and pull simultaneously caused the door to give way, and she fell forward and found herself hanging head first out of the carriage.

"What have we here?" a gruff voice asked.

Bridget closed her eyes trying to force air into her compressed lungs. "Please, sir, you must help me. I am being held against my will." She turned her head as much as she was able to plead with her eyes. "Could you untie my hands?"

"Seems to me you got in the cab willingly enough. The gent said as you were his wife."

"I am not his wife, but his cousin!"

"I can help you back upright, but I don't plan on getting between you an' 'im."

"That much would be appreciated." The man righted her and she sat on the floor of the coach, which was none too clean, while she caught her breath. The door shut with a click behind her, before she could stop it.

It would be her own guile versus Rory's strength, it seemed. She wriggled herself back up to the seat and was almost composed again when the door opened. Aunt Betha was standing in the opening, looking pleased with herself. She climbed in with a little help from Riordan.

Bridget scowled at him when he entered and sat beside his mother.

"Are you not pleased to see me, niece?"

"I was led to believe you were at Dungarvan," she answered in clipped tones. If Riordan was required to marry her to receive his full inheritance, then they would not kill her, at least. At this point, she would put little else past them. Her aunt had moved with more dexterity than she had in Ireland. Had it all been an act?

"Riordan tells me you have come to your senses and agreed to marry him," she said with a tone of satisfaction.

"Only on the condition that it be a marriage in name only and I may live where and how I wish. Would you mind loosening the ropes, Rory? I am losing sensation in my arms and hands."

Bridget could feel her aunt's eyes narrow at her while she turned her back for Riordan to undo the ropes.

"I no longer think you are in a position to negotiate, my dear."

We will see about that, Bridget said to herself. She did not want to speak any more. It was difficult to maintain her composure, especially now that she realized what a horrid mistake she had made. She had never been naïve, but neither had she come across the likes of someone so deceptive as her aunt. Her mistake had been in trusting Rory and whatever hold his mother had over him. She tried to lean against the side of the carriage and ignore them, but her aunt persisted.

"I trust you have brought all of your belongings with you?"

Why would her aunt ask such a thing? Bridget's mind began to work furiously. "I have very little in the way of possessions, Aunt," she replied in a suspect manner, though accurately.

"You will search her trunks as soon as we reach the port," her aunt commanded.

So they were the ones to have, at the very least, ransacked her house. Whatever they were searching for, they had not found, evidently.

"You stole my dowry," Bridget seethed.

"Of course I took it, because you are to marry him," her aunt replied.

"When? My father had no idea."

"Of course he didn't. He never thought to look. It has been gone for years. Your cousin has very expensive habits."

"There was never any agreement between us."

"That is true, Mother. I did not know you had taken money from her." Riordan spoke up.

"You are welcome to pay her back," she snapped. "If it were not for you and your ways, we would not be so desperate. Do you think I want you to be forced to marry her?"

"In a word, yes." He did not hide his sarcasm.

"Without the income from the other properties, Dungarvan and its name will sink."

"To be fair, I inherited a great deal of debt. I cannot shoulder the entire blame for it."

"That is true, and why I am helping you solve this now," she retorted.

"What is it you are searching for? I have nothing left," Bridget said with absolute disgust.

"You are not as bright as I took you for if you believe that. How much farther to the coast?" Her aunt glared, changing the subject. "These old bones do not enjoy cheap excuses for carriages."

"A fair distance, I am afraid," Riordan muttered.

The two of them began to argue about what had brought them to this point, and Bridget did her utmost to shut it out. How could she have been so stupid? She had walked into a trap—if not that night, he would have found her eventually. There was a little doubt in her mind that she would be forced into this marriage before anyone thought to look for her.

As if her wounds were not already open, a storm blew up and their pace was forced to slow to a crawl as the roads became soaked and muddy. The carriage rocked too and fro as wind and sheets of rain battered it. Reluctantly, she felt for the driver, but more so for the horses.

A clap of thunder shook the earth beneath them and the horses lurched in their traces, causing the carriage to tip at an angle before righting itself. Riordan was apparently prone to feel ill with too much motion and they were forced to stop the carriage so he could be sick. He thrust open the door and a cold gust of wet wind filled the compartment. It flew shut with a bang.

When he had finished emptying the contents of his stomach, he climbed back in drenched to the bone, holding his middle.

Aunt Betha shook her head.

The carriage began to lurch forward and then rocked back into a rut with a thud. Sounds of the driver yelling at the horses could be heard even through the heavy rain.

"What is going on?" Aunt Betha demanded.

"It appears that the horses are unable to pull the carriage from the mud," Riordan drawled.

"Stupid boy! What will you do when I am not here to get you out of every fix?"

Bridget wondered how she planned to fix this.

"I assume I will sink or swim," he muttered with a heavy sigh. "I will go and see if there is a nearby inn or someone who can provide shelter for the night."

"Yes, you do that," she said in an acerbic tone, as though he had done this purposefully.

Bridget could almost feel sorry for him, but she had little emotion left to spare.

CHAPTER 20

Tobin and Waverley arrived at Dungarvan's house on Albermarle Street only to find it deserted.

"By God, he has kidnapped her!" Tobin growled. "When I get my hands on him he will pay for this and then he will pay for everything he ever did to me."

"Let us see if we can discover where they might have gone. With the storm brewing, they might not be far. I would not set out in this weather. The carriage would be stuck before it had covered above a stage or two." Waverley's voice was far too calm and composed.

Tobin grunted. "You give Dungarvan too much credit."

"We are absolutely certain she went with him?" Waverley looked sideways at him.

"According to one of the grooms. He saw her get into a hackney with Dungarvan in the back alley. I bet he decided to abscond with her back to Ireland like a spider up a drainpipe."

"And risk their necks in this weather?"

"He knows I will come after her. He probably thinks they will be aboard ship before we notice she is gone."

"I do not fancy a trip to Portsmouth in a storm," Waverley grumbled.

"You do not have to go, sir. This is my battle to fight."

"I cannot believe you even said that to me." Waverley looked incredulous.

"Let us waste no more time, then." They rode back to Waverley Place; thankfully the guests were all gone or retired for the night. Meg was waiting up for them in the study, along with Lord and Lady Wrexford.

"You did not find her?" the Duchess asked.

"The house was deserted. We think he is taking her to Portsmouth, with the intention of reaching Ireland as soon as possible."

"I will have the carriage readied," Waverley declared, crossing to the bell-rope.

"I am going with you," Wrexford said. "This is partly my fault for pushing to have matters resolved so quickly."

"It is hardly your fault, sir. If her relations were not rotten to the core, none of this would have happened. All I care about now is finding her before it is too late."

Tobin and Waverley set off on horseback since it would be easier to search that way. Wrexford was to follow more slowly in the carriage. Tobin was quite certain Dungarvan was not inventive enough to take a circuitous route, assuming he thought they had a whole night's advantage before discovery.

They achieved two hours in the saddle before the storm hit in earnest. "They cannot be much further ahead. A carriage could not move very fast at all in this," Tobin shouted over the battering wind as the rain struck them in sideways sheets.

"Perhaps they sought shelter somewhere," Waverley reasoned, "although I have not seen anywhere for miles that would have room to stable a coach."

"Guildford should not be too much further. We can wait the storm out there."

Tobin lifted his collar and shrugged his shoulder to his ear to try to shield his bare skin from the worst of the rain. It was shocking how much it hurt when you were going at any speed. The roads were growing more treacherous by the minute as the ruts filled with water and they were forced to slow down.

"Up ahead!" Waverley called. "It looks like a coach."

Tobin prayed it was them and Bridget was unharmed. He could not say as much for Dungarvan. He would be fortunate to see the night through once Tobin was finished with him. As they pulled up alongside the coach, they saw that the horses had been unhitched. Tobin rode up to the window and peered inside.

"It is empty," he said, feeling his heart sink to his toes. "They cannot be too much further. No one would want to ride carriage horses very far. There would have been at least three of them, if you count the coachman, so someone had to walk."

Waverley opened the boot. "There are trunks in here. We can come back for those."

They forged on to the next village that boasted a coaching inn— another two miles. Tobin was not in the mood to deal with any of this. It was somewhere in the wee hours of the morning and he was soaked to the skin. He had not been in the saddle this long since Waterloo, and his injuries were screaming from the exertion.

Waverley dismounted and tossed Tobin the reins while he went to the door. He pounded loudly on the solid wood, but no one answered.

"Come around the back. They cannot have been far ahead of us."

Waverley led his horse and Tobin followed. There was no one in the yard, so the Duke took the liberty of opening the stable door and leading his mount inside. Again, Tobin followed. There they found a soaked driver rubbing down two horses.

"Are you the jarvey of the coach that was stuck in the mire a couple of miles past?"

"Aye," he grunted, looking none too pleased.

"Were your passengers a gentleman and a lady?"

"Two ladies." The weathered man continued to chew on a piece of grass and did not bother to look up.

"A gentleman and two ladies?" Waverley asked, growing impatient.

"I just said so, didn't I?"

"Are they inside the inn?"

He shrugged carelessly. "The old lady would not have gone too far."

Tobin led the horses to stalls while listening to this exchange and tossed both horses an armful of hay before following Waverley into the inn. The back door was unlocked and, being a Duke, he walked straight in and came face to face with a stunned innkeeper.

"I'm sorry, your lordship, but I have no more room. I just took in some travellers who were caught in the storm."

"I am interested in the travellers, not a room. The young lady is being held against her will."

The innkeeper looked suspicious. "His lordship said as how they were married. They have an old lady with them."

Waverley pulled out his card and handed it to the man, whose eyes grew wide. "I don't want no trouble, your Grace, begging your pardon."

"Nor do I, sir, but a grievous wrong is being committed and it is our duty to see it put right."

"Of course, your Grace."

"First, I want to know where the man is," Tobin growled.

The innkeeper paused with warranted hesitation before pointing across the tap-room. "He is in the parlour, having a drink."

Waverley put a hand on Tobin's arm as if to restrain him.

"He is mine," Tobin growled and marched across the room.

Tobin flung open the door. Dungarvan was lounging before a roaring fire, his eyes half closed, the remains of a meal cluttered a small table near the one leaded window.

Grabbing him by the neckcloth, Tobin slammed his fist into the man's face, drawing his cork before Dungarvan realized who or what had hit him.

"If it isn't O'Neill," Riordan slurred. "You were quite unexpected."

"You always did underestimate me," Tobin hissed as he took Riordan's neck between his hands.

"She came with me willingly and has agreed to marry me," Dungarvan said with a gleam of satisfaction. He was remarkably calm and collected, considering Tobin could snap his neck at any moment.

"I do not believe you." Tobin knew all of this rogue's tricks.

"Suit yourself. You may ask her if you can remove your hands from my person long enough," he choked out.

There was just enough sincerity in Riordan's eyes that Tobin loosened his grip. It was just long enough for his opponent to swing his arm and land a decent punch to his stomach.

"Oof," Tobin grunted. "Just like old times, ye devil, except this time it is two in my favour." They circled each other like drunken sailors just before an unholy brawl broke out.

Waverley was staying out of it—for now. He would never take away Tobin's chance to vindicate himself. From the corner of his eye, Tobin saw him trying to remove objects from their path of destruction. He was only mildly successful as Tobin launched himself at Riordan and they went flying across a table holding the remains of Dungarvan's supper. Crockery, glassware and cutlery crashed to the floor and Tobin found himself lying on top of his adversary in the middle of this chaos, the table legs having snapped. Riordan groaned and, caring nothing for the rules of gentlemen, Tobin dealt him a heavy blow to the jaw for good measure.

"Get up, ye blackguard," Tobin snarled, jumping to his feet. "It isn't as amusing when it is one on one, is it?" He bent forward, reaching down to drag Riordan to his feet.

In the next second his legs shot from beneath him and he went sprawling backwards, brought down by a scything kick. Dungarvan leaped to his feet, snatched up a chair and swung it at Tobin's head. At the last moment, Tobin rolled sideways and they closed together, punches flailing wildly, each of them ducking and swerving. Riordan caught Tobin a spanker across the side of his head; responding with a doubler to the man's abdomen, Tobin won a foot of space. Swift as an Irish leprechaun, he threw Dungarvan a cross buttock and fell on him before the devil could retaliate. He landed two knuckle-crunching blows before Waverley's hand caught his arm.

"I think you have made your point."

"A point is entirely unnecessary, isn't it, Rory?" Tobin held his hand back ready to strike.

"You always did fight like a gutter rat, which is where you belong," Riordan spat.

"The gutter is better than Hell, where I am happy to send you now so you and Kilmorgan can rot together."

He was breathing hard, but Dungarvan was panting the harder. They glared at each other, the years and years of hatred spilling forth unchecked. Suddenly Tobin saw the man for what he was—a miserable, spineless piece of dung. He slammed Riordan's head down for good measure and stood up. "Ye aren't worth it."

"*Go hifreann leat!*" Riordan spat, lying supine on the floorboards.

"Likewise. Now where the devil is my betrothed?" Tobin barked.

AN UNHOLY FRACAS had been taking place in the room below her, and Bridget sat shaking with fear. It had happened from time to time with men in the army, and she found such brawls almost worse than battle. She began to pray that the drunken louts would leave so she could finally try to rest. Her head was pounding, her heart was bruised, and she needed quiet to settle her mind—if that were even a possibility. Her aunt was a formidable opponent and did not play fair. She would be hard to outwit.

The noise from downstairs grew louder, and the voice now echoing through the inn was unmistakable.

Bridget gasped. "Tobin?" she asked out loud. Putting down her hair pins, she opened the door and ran down the stairs. She could hear them arguing.

"Go on and ask her if I forced her," Rory taunted and Bridget felt herself cringe. She was close enough now to see the two men as she crossed the empty tap-room. They had obviously been fighting. Riordan was holding a bloodied handkerchief to his nose and Tobin was holding his fist to his chest. Bridget could see his knuckles were also bleeding. Tobin was angry and she feared he might hurt Riordan again. Bridget had not immediately noticed Waverley standing in the corner, but then he turned his head, catching her attention. He raised his brows at her in silent enquiry. She shook her head.

"I spoke to my cousin after you evicted me from the ball. She chased after me, in fact. She said she had released you from the betrothal," Riordan was gaining in confidence as he propped himself against the wall and folded his hands over his chest.

"Her maid said she was to take a position in Norfolk; then we found a letter turning the position down."

"Yes, because she decided to come with me and marry."

Tobin stood rigid, glaring at her cousin. Bridget felt his pain as her own as she watched the agony in his eyes.

"Whether or not you hate me, I need to find her. I need to know she is safe, and that she is with you of her own free will." Tobin's voice cracked and Bridget's heart along with it. "If she chooses you, I will walk away."

"Why did she break the betrothal?" Riordan asked, as though they had not just been beating each other to flinders. Gentlemen were so strange.

Tobin began to stride about the small parlour. "Because I am an ejeet, and did not tell her how I truly felt," he muttered. "She was just trying to do what was best for me. She said something about being too far apart in stations and not needing to marry for convenience any more. It was all nonsense, of course."

"Then why was she looking for a position?" Rory was not making this easy for Tobin, or herself, Bridget thought, but they were good questions.

"I could not tell you," Tobin answered, running his hand through his hair. "Even more curious is why she gave up the position and ran to you when she wanted to marry me in the first place to avoid marriage to you."

Rory shrugged, suddenly looking defeated. "I want to know that you deserve her."

"Who could deserve her? She is the most beautiful, extraordinary, giving person I have ever met. You and I are not fit to wash her boots."

Bridget's throat burned with unshed emotion.

"Do you love her?"

"Aye, more than anyone or anything on this earth," Tobin answered in a strangled voice. He was trying not to cry. "The thought of doing this without her..."

"Have you told her this?"

"He just did," Bridget said as she began to walk into the room. It was undoubtedly the wrong thing to do, but her feet seemed to be moving of their own volition.

Tobin met her and pulled her into his arms. "Are you daft, woman? How could you leave me?"

"I was trying to do what was best for you, Tobin."

"You would prefer him to me?" He inclined his head towards Riordan, but did not take his eyes from her. Their heat bored straight through her.

"No need to answer that," Riordan said dryly.

"You are what is best for me, lass. Please say you will marry me, *a chuisle, a chroí*. I only discovered you had left so soon because I was coming to find you to announce our betrothal."

"Are you sure you have thought properly about this? There are so many reasons why we should not," she argued half-heartedly.

"Name one that holds water. I cannot think of any—and I do not want to hear anything about the bloody title or money."

"Well, I care about it," Lady Dungarvan snarled from the door. All of them gasped and turned, surprised by her entrance. She was holding a pistol, aimed right at Bridget. "Now give me the key, you stupid chit!"

"Wh-what key?" Bridget had no notion of a key.

"The one mentioned in your father's will!" Her hand was shaking as she held the gun.

"Aunt, this is truly the first I have heard of it. If I may see the will, perhaps it will become clearer to me." Bridget did her best to keep her voice neutral and not antagonistic.

"I am losing my patience, gel. It said the 'key of my heart holds my greatest treasure.'"

Bridget frowned in thought. Trust her father to write in riddles.

Perhaps he had done it to protect her from his family. However that may be, she did not know what it meant.

Lady Dungarvan let out a howl of frustration. "Rory, go back to the coach and fetch her trunks at once!"

Bridget tried not to laugh at the absurd look on her cousin's face. A movement behind her aunt caused Bridget to blink, but she tried to keep her face impassive. Lord Wrexford had arrived and was creeping up behind Lady Dungarvan, who still had her back to the door. Fortunately, she was too distracted by ordering her son about to notice she was about to be overtaken.

Surprising the old woman, Lord Wrexford wrapped his arms around hers and pulled her backwards. The gun exploded with a roar, deafening in the small room, the ball going harmlessly into the ceiling. A cloud of plaster dusted the combatants. Waverley sprang to Wrexford's aid. Aunt Betha was no match for the two men and was soon subdued, at least physically.

"Unhand me, you English oaf! How dare you interfere? Riordan, do something, you snivelling man-milliner," she wailed. "Too think how I have strived to make a man of you. And you!" She spat in Bridget's direction. "Viper! Jade! Turncoat! You have not heard the last of this..."

Her wails and shouts fell on deaf ears. "Stubble it, woman, or I will gag you!" Waverley warned.

Bridget glanced sideways to see if her cousin would come to his mother's rescue, but he seemed to sag with relief.

"What will you do with her?" Rory finally asked.

Waverley frowned in thought. "I think the four of us can devise something satisfactory amongst us, to keep this quiet, but she cannot be allowed to go free. It is clear she is a threat to Miss Murphy."

Her aunt squirmed, trying to fight Waverley's hold.

"Perhaps house arrest at Dungarvan; and ensuring that whatever was stolen is returned to Miss Murphy," Wrexford suggested.

"I stole nothing! That money belonged to the Murphy family!"

"Hush, woman!" Wrexford snapped.

"That is far greater leniency than you deserve, Mother," Riordan said with impatience.

"And ye are a saint she leads about by yer nose," Tobin growled.

"Might I suggest you both go upstairs? I will see you locked in your rooms and safely on your way to Ireland in the morning." As Waverley escorted Riordan and Lady Dungarvan away, Bridget felt Tobin's hands on her. She leaned against him with relief.

"Do you know what key she was talking about?"

"I do not have any idea. She seemed to think it was in my possession."

"I retrieved your trunks from the abandoned coach," Wrexford said. "They are safe for now."

"Thank you, my lord."

"I will go and see if Waverley needs my assistance." He gave a brief smile and closed the door behind him.

Tobin pulled Bridget with him to a chair that had been pushed against the wall.

"I am fashed," he said as he sat her sideways across his lap.

"Are you hurt?"

"He managed only one good hit," Tobin replied. "I am more exhausted over you."

"I did not mean for it to come to this," she whispered.

Looking into his eyes, she saw his vulnerability and love. She had mistaken his lack of expressed affection for a change in his feelings.

"Ye... ye are... unharmed, Bridget?" he murmured, his voice hoarse. Concern rippled through the rough tone. "I will drag him behind my horse by his—"

"Shh." Reaching up, she tenderly fingered a cut above one of his eyebrows. "More so than you, it seems, my *anamchara*. He did me no more harm than tie my hands, so you may be easy."

He brushed a stray curl back from her forehead and gazed down at her. His green eyes drilled into her but he said not a word.

"Tobin?"

"Yes, *mo grá?*"

"I want more than friendship. *Tá mo chroí istigh ionat.*"

"Thank God for that. My heart has been yours since I first saw you." The words were strangled, as though they had been locked in his throat. A slow smile slid across his face, and lifting one hand to stroke her cheek with his thumb, he bent and softly touched his lips to hers. Warmth flooded her being and at once paraded her love in her cheeks.

"You really must stop behaving like a ruffian, you know. That cut will need a stitch. You cannot beat every man who crosses my path. When will you get it into your thick, Irish skull that I love you too much to keep seeing you hurt?" she demanded as he straightened.

"Thank God for that," Tobin said again. Without warning, he pulled her to him and took her mouth in a fiery, passionate kiss, erasing all doubts—and most thoughts—from her mind. When at last he pulled away, he favoured her with his devilish grin and remarked wickedly, "I told ye I was no' a gentleman."

"Thank God for that!"

EPILOGUE

Six weeks later...

It was so strange to be preparing for her wedding without any of her family present. It was bittersweet. It had taken some time to clear matters up in London, but they had sold her family's town house and brought everything back to Ireland. Tobin had sold out of the army in order to take over his duties as Kilmorgan.

The ceremony would be small, with only Lord and Lady Wrexford and the Duke and Duchess of Waverley in attendance. Bridget was still in mourning but there was no reason to delay the wedding, since she was living at Wrexford.

She wore her mother's pale blue silk gown. The old lace had been replaced with a beautiful Mechlin lace which the Duchess had purchased in Belgium as a wedding gift. It would not do to wear black to her own wedding. No indeed. Maria had styled her hair into curls, with half pinned up and half allowed to fall over her shoulders in a very soft manner.

A gentle knock on the door was preceded by the Duchess peeping into her room.

"Am I disturbing you? You look perfect!" she exclaimed.

"The dress is more beautiful than I could have imagined. Thank you."

"It was my pleasure." She held out a thick pouch. "This was delivered for you from Dungarvan. We have been debating whether or not to give it to you before the ceremony."

"I shall not be thrown into a fit of the blue-devil, I assure you. I doubt anything they say can alter my feelings at the moment."

"I will leave the decision to you then. We will look for you in a few minutes. We are leaving for the church now."

The Duchess left quietly and Bridget stared at the packet for a few minutes before deciding to open it. It contained a sheaf of papers, on the top of which was a letter addressed to her.

Dearest cousin,

I hope that some time has healed your opinion of me. I do not have good reasons for my actions against you, except I have never been strong enough to withstand Mother. She has always ruled with an iron fist, as you know. Nevertheless, I was able to obtain your father's will from her; please find it with this letter. I hope that one day you will find it in your heart to forgive me. I have begun the process of repaying your dowry. Thus far, I have found no other evidence of anything Mother has stolen. Please correct me if there are further wrongs I need to right. I hope this eases your mind and that you find the treasure you were looking for. My felicitations upon the occasion of your wedding.

Your devoted cousin,
Riordan

Bridget wiped away a tear which had spilled over. She had known in her heart that Rory was not evil, but he had always been easily influenced by others. Bridget had been able to escape his mother's clutches, but he had not. At least he was now trying to do what was right, although it did not excuse his ill behaviour towards Tobin.

She rifled through the will, but there was hardly time to look before she left for the wedding. There was a little doubt in her mind that there was any monetary treasure to be had. Father would have told her if he had acquired some great windfall. She shook her head and laughed when, scanning the pages for those words, she found them at last.

To my daughter, Bridget, the key of my heart holds my greatest treasure.

What could they mean? Now was certainly not the time to ponder her father's riddles. She went to her mother's jewellery case to find her pearls; there was nothing she would rather wear on this most special of occasions. She pulled out the pouch which held the string of pearls and matching earrings and poured the contents into her hand. To her surprise, a small key also dropped into her palm. Laughing, Bridget set it on the dressing table and put on the pearls so she would be prepared when the Duke came for her. Her curiosity was now running rampant.

She searched the small case for somewhere into which the key could fit, now suspicious after discovering the secret panel in her father's desk.

Sure enough, a panel was hidden under a piece of velvet in the bottom of the case and the key fit perfectly into the hole.

Bridget let out a gasp when she saw what was inside.

There was another small velvet pouch, and it contained a small fortune in jewels. There was a miniature of her mother and father as they must have looked at their wedding, and at the very bottom was a packet of letters tied up with a narrow ribbon. They appeared to be letters her parents must have exchanged. She held the picture and letters to her heart, inhaling her mother's nostalgic scent. She would treasure these later, she mused, for another knock on the door indicated it was time to go. Hurriedly she replaced the treasure and locked the jewels back in the hidden panel.

Walking over to the door, she opened it to see the Duke waiting for her.

"Are you ready?" he asked.

"I am." She smiled.

"Tobin is a very lucky man," he said as he led her through the house and to the small family chapel between the house and the cliffs.

As they entered the small church and she saw Tobin waiting for her by the altar, she knew that it was she who was the lucky one— especially when she saw that devilish smile and green eyes twinkling at her.

"*Beggorah mo grá*," Tobin said reverently as he took her hand from the Duke's and tucked it under his arm near his chest.

"Dearly beloved," the vicar began, but Bridget scarcely heard a word, she was near to bursting with happiness. The only thing she could think was that the greatest treasure had been with her the whole time.

AFTERWORD

Author's note: British spellings and grammar have been used in an effort to reflect what would have been done in the time period in which the novels are set. While I realize all words may not be exact, I hope you can appreciate the differences and effort made to be historically accurate while attempting to retain readability for the modern audience.

Thank you for reading *An Officer, Not a Gentleman*. I hope you enjoyed it. If you did, please help other readers find this book:

1. This ebook is lendable, so send it to a friend who you think might like it so she or he can discover me, too.
2. Help other people find this book by writing a review.
3. Sign up for my new releases at www.Elizabethjohnsauthor.com, so you can find out about the next book as soon as it's available.
4. Connect with me at any of these places:

www.Elizabethjohnsauthor.com
Facebook

Instagram
Amazon
Bookbub
Goodreads
elizabethjohnsauthor@gmail.com

ACKNOWLEDGMENTS

There are many, many people who have contributed to making my books possible.

My family, who deals with the idiosyncrasies of a writer's life that do not fit into a 9 to 5 work day.

Dad, who reads every single version before and after anyone else—that alone qualifies him for sainthood.

Wilette and Anj, who take my visions and interprets them, making them into works of art people open in the first place.

My team of friends who care about my stories enough to help me shape them before everyone else sees them.

Heather who helps me say what I mean to!

And to the readers who make all of this possible.
I am forever grateful to you all.

ALSO BY ELIZABETH JOHNS

Made in the USA
Las Vegas, NV
23 September 2022